Fortune's Well, Book One:

Hangman's Revenge

By Chantelle Atkins & Sim Alec Sansford

Disclaimer

Note from the Authors

This story came about in a rather unusual way.

Having already worked together for a while running Chasing Driftwood Writing Group, Sim randomly asked me one day if I had ever considered writing with another author. The short answer was no - this was certainly never something that had crossed my mind. I had no idea how such a thing would work. But Sim had a title and a vague idea and fancied throwing that idea back and forth a bit between us to see what could happen.

I was instantly attracted to the idea of writing together for two reasons. One, Sim and I get on so well as friends and business partners, and two, I was curious! This was brand new to me and I thought, why not? It will be good experience.

It seemed to just spiral from there. A few ideas jumped between messages and suddenly I had an idea for a male character and Sim had one for a female. I wrote the first chapter having no real clue if it was what Sim had in mind or not and he responded with his. Off we went! Chapters started flying back and forth very quickly and before we knew it we had a real story on our hands, one that kept changing and developing and twisting as we wrote it.

We very rarely got stuck. We seemed to keep each other motivated and excited to keep writing. There was no real planning either, which is unusual for me, but somehow it all seemed to happen in messenger! As we neared the end of book 1 we already had ideas for a trilogy and we just kept going with it. Looking at the finished book now, I really can't quite believe we did it. I'm so glad we did though. Our writing styles mesh well together and we both fell in love with JJ and Darcie to the extent I think these characters will pop up again somewhere further down the line…

Chantelle Atkins

Wow. Did we really just write an entire trilogy via social media messages? Short answer - yes.

As Chantelle explained, the initial idea for this book came to me first. I wanted to create a story where the underdogs could use their anxieties, experiences, and anything that would normally be a negative and turn it into something magical and glorious.

The initial title, *A Jar Full of Empty*, came to me one evening out of the blue. I was trying to figure out a way of explaining how I was feeling at the time and that seemed to capture it perfectly. From there, sparks of an idea began to form.

I knew I could never do it justice on my own though. I needed someone who's writing was deep, and dark, and edgy, and real. That person was Chantelle Atkins. I prayed she would agree and I was blown away when she said yes.

The first chapter she sent was absolutely perfect, and pretty much remains exactly as it is in the final book. Co-writing was a fantastic process - I got to be a writer and a reader! Never knowing where Chantelle would take the story next.

Chapter by chapter we went, and before we even knew what had happened we'd completed three books over the course of 11 months.

Like the mysterious mist haunting JJ Carson, the story shifted and changed. It took on a life of its own. It teased sequels and prequels. It grew and expanded.

It inspired me. It inspired Chantelle.

And I hope that now it will inspire you too.

Sim Alec Sansford

Dedication

This book is for anyone who has ever felt misunderstood.
We see you.

"Don't worry about the darkness in my soul.

It ignites me like an embered coal."

-Anonymous.

1: JJ

The jar on the dresser is empty.

This is not good.

The last thing my mother said to me before she was locked up for killing my dad was this: 'This jar used to be my mother's and then it was mine and the most important thing about it is you can never let it sit empty. You must always keep it full, okay? Or you'll invoke the curse and get the bad family luck.' When I started to shake my head, she frowned and pointed a finger into my face. 'Don't give me that look. You *must* take it seriously. I'm going away for a while and you'll take the jar and look after it for me. You keep it full, you understand? I used to keep flowers in it. Dried ones, fresh ones, dead ones. Sometimes just petals floating in the water. You can keep whatever you like in it so long as it's something that makes you smile. You must *never* let it be empty JJ, otherwise, you know what will happen?'

I'd shook my head at her, and my eyes had started to sting at the thought of her leaving me. 'Never let it get empty JJ or the empty will get *you*.'

And now there it is, the jar my mother cared so much about, sat on the dresser in my bedroom in Uncle Henry's house. Empty. I'm getting ready for school - the last day before the summer, the day I sit my final exam - I'm straightening my tie and looking in the mirror when I notice the jar. It's one of those big, chunky mason jars, with a clip lid. After my mum left, I filled it with marbles.

Then I'd filled it with pennies. And after they'd sat there for about a year or so, I filled it with sweets from Halloween. The last thing I had in the jar was a bunch of dead dandelions. I don't know what made me fill it with them. Maybe it was thinking about my mum after the last visit, seeing the dandelion yellow of her hair and missing her so badly when I got home, that my guts ached with it.

Dead dandelions, but now they are gone.

I stand and stare and wonder if what she said was true. I've got a few minutes to spare, so I take my notebook out of the dresser drawer and place it next to the empty jar. I grab a pencil and start to sketch it, my tongue stuck out the corner of my mouth. My mum used to laugh when I did that, but I never realise I'm doing it until someone points it out.

I'm halfway through drawing the empty jar when my bedroom door bursts open and Uncle Henry barges in. Uncle Henry never knocks, mainly because this is his house and he can do what the hell he likes, but partly because he does not trust me. Not one little bit. He looks at me sketching the jar and he frowns and puffs out his chest and narrows his bright blue eyes.

'What's all this crap?'

Everything is crap to Uncle Henry. Uncle Henry does not think much of anything. As far as I can tell the only things he cares about are drink and women, followed maybe by his German Shepherd, Chester. I've lived here on the farm with him since I was ten years old. It was bad from the start. He took me in because he had to - because there was nowhere else for me to go and because I was his brother's kid. The main problem is I look too much like my mother and in his eyes my mother is crazy.

'Nothing,' I say, sweeping my pencils and notebook into the drawer and pushing it shut. I want to ask him where the dandelions went but I don't dare. The best way to avoid annoying him is to give him what he wants the most - for me not to exist.

'Load of dead flowers in there,' he says then, answering the question for me. 'What the hell was that about?'

He's looking at me the way he always does - with suspicion and resentment. My Uncle Henry is a very handsome man, by the way. He is tall and muscly from all the work on the farm. He has dark blonde hair, short on the sides and back and longer on top. He has long eyelashes and full lips. He looks like a movie star, no kidding. And he knows it. And all the women around here think he is an angel, looking like that and taking me in.

I shrug, knowing that he wouldn't want to hear what Mum told me about her special jar.

'Dead flowers?' he says for me, eyebrows raised. Then he does the thing when he looks me up and down slowly as if trying to figure me out. His nostrils twitch when he does it, like he can't even stand the smell of me. 'Jesus Christ JJ,' he says as he leaves, 'no wonder nobody likes you.'

I leave the house after that. Shoulder my backpack and trudge across the dusty farmyard towards the open gate. On one side of the house is a busy road, cars and trucks and tractors sailing by constantly, and on the other are miles and miles of open fields. Uncle Henry owns five acres of them and aside from potatoes, he mostly keeps them full of cows. He inherited them from his parents. Both he and my father grew up on this farm and sometimes when he's had a few drinks and a lady friend has made him feel especially happy, Uncle Henry tells me stories about their childhood. They are all good ones: he and my dad searching for Easter eggs in the barn; the day they both climbed on the tyre swing and they were too heavy, so the rope broke, and they rolled down the hill together; or the time they saved an orphaned calf and brought it back to life.

He says the good times ended when my mother came on the scene. I don't know too much about it, but I do know he resented and distrusted her from the start. My mother might talk about family curses but to Uncle Henry it is far simpler than that. Madness runs in her family, he says. It touched her mother and her father before her, and it touched my mum and the reason he can't stand to look at me too long is because he thinks it's touched me too.

On the other side of the gate, I cross the road and trot down the riverside path that will eventually take me to school. It's a beautiful route - the winding river green and gold as the sun slants through the trees that line it, birds singing and the smell of a long summer in the air. It's beautiful and I love to bring my notebook down here, but on the way to school I hate it. If there was another route to take, even a longer one, I would leave home earlier and take it. But there isn't.

On the last day of school, I feel the trouble building around me like storm clouds. My guts are a mess by the time I get there because I know I am not off the hook yet. I might have made it this far, but I still have to get home again, and that's when they will strike.

Uncle Henry was right about nobody liking me. It's true and I think it embarrasses him because he's always been so popular. He tries to give me tips sometimes. Take off your glasses, stand up straight, look people in the eye and don't take any crap, that kind of thing. He taught me some moves too, just in case.

I haven't made a friend since I moved here six years ago. The trouble with small towns is everyone knows each other and because everyone knows Uncle Henry, everyone knows my mum, so of course everyone knows that she flipped one day and killed my dad.

For the last six years the best reactions I've had from people have been endless, probing questions about why she did it and how she did it and the worst reactions I've had have been the fights. I say fights because I try and fight back, like Uncle Henry tells me to. He'd hate me even more if I just took it. And maybe if it were a fair fight, one on one, I might stand a chance.

But what happens today after the final exam that sets me free, is what happens at least three times a week. Sometimes they jump me on the way there, sometimes they make me wait all day wondering if it will happen on the way home. I've tried hiding, I've tried running, I've tried staying behind at school and one time I even took a knife with me and tried threatening them.

That didn't go so well. They told their parents and Uncle Henry was absolutely livid. Maybe that's when he started to distrust me.

'If you ever do anything like that again I'll have you locked up like your mother!' he yelled.

But he doesn't want me to just take it?

I can't win. And here they are. As predicted. The gruesome threesome I know and loathe so well. Jared Wheeler, Andrew Hart and Frankie Simpson. They are all in my year. They are all bigger than me. They all have shaved heads and facial hair. They all play rugby at the weekend. They are leaning against the trees, kicking up dust, killing time until I come along.

'Shit,' I mutter and slip my backpack off my shoulders.

'All right crazy boy,' sneers Jared, the ringleader, with his pierced ear and rolled up sleeves. Jared is a sly one. You never see him coming and I'm not kidding. It's like he can materialise out of thin air. There one minute, gone the next. You can never let your guard down with him, never. Today he is grinning like I am some sort of grand prize. 'Last day of school, so we're gonna give you a beating you'll remember all summer.'

The others chuckle and snigger like hyenas and I put up my fists.

Later, when I stagger home, muddied, and bloodied with one strap on my backpack broken Uncle Henry throws down his newspaper and jumps to his feet. He points out of the door and I know he is pointing to the barn.

'Jesus Christ JJ, get in that barn, I'm gonna teach you how to defend yourself if it's the last thing I bloody do!'

So, the last day of school, before the first day of summer, I am standing in the barn, with hay dust circling in the air around me and Uncle Henry is pulling up my fists and holding them steady, and when my feet aren't positioned right, he's kicking them into place, and I'm thinking, Mum was right, she was right. I didn't look after her jar… I didn't put anything in it that made me smile and now the empty has got me because I swear that is all I can ever feel. Emptiness.

2: Darcie

Here I am, enjoying the last few tendrils of some pleasant dream I already can't remember. From downstairs I hear my mother's voice, like nails on a chalkboard, clawing inside my ears.

'Darcie, dear. School.'

I let out a heavy sigh before answering. 'I'm up, Mom.' No response.

She probably feels like she's fulfilled her maternal duties for the day. I stretch my arms high above my head and yawn, before pulling myself from the safety of the duvet. Downstairs I can hear my mother's shrill voice once again. This time she's berating our housekeeper, Julia, over the way she's folded the napkins. As if it matters. I mean honestly, in the grand scheme of things does it really make a difference whether your napkins are round, square, or itsy-bitsy triangles? Who knows, maybe.

I shower in record time, dry myself off in front of the full-length mirror outside the en suite, and frown as I examine my body. I chew my bottom lip with uncertainty as I turn from right to left and back again. Pinching the skin of my hips and sighing, until my eyes drift across to my belly button and I smile at the ocean blue stud. Though I had never been a fan of piercings in anywhere other than the ears, I got this one last year behind my parents' backs. It was my little secret, just for me. My one taste of rebellion, or "Rebellyon" as my friend Vicky had called it. I laugh out loud. *That was dumb.*

I slip into my blue and white checked summer dress, charcoal blazer embossed with the school logo and regulation shoes. Taking one final look in the mirror, I scrape my hair back into a high ponytail that falls down my neck with a soft curl at the end. The framed photo of my aunt Jenna on the nightstand catches my eye in the reflection. I miss her so damn much it hurts. In fact, every time I think about her a lump so big rises in my throat that I fear I might choke.

I look a lot like Jenna, long golden hair, milky smooth skin, and deep blue eyes. She was my father's sister, and we were pretty much inseparable until she died when I was twelve. The funeral was back home in Orange County, so I never got to go. My parents wouldn't allow it. Funerals were "no place for children", so my younger brother, Jeremy, and I were off the guest list.

'Wish me luck,' I whisper into the empty. Today is the last day of school before the summer break. Just one more exam, and one more day of nodding and smiling, laughing where appropriate and pretending I gave a damn about makeup, shoes and whatever the hell Kim and Kanye are up to these days. My words were intended for Jenna but from the doorway my mother answers.

'Luck with what, Darling?'

'Oh, I...'

Before I have a chance to finish my thought, she has scurried over to stand behind me in the mirror, straightening up my blazer and smoothing out my hair.

'Don't forget, your father is back tonight. I want you and your brother home on time, okay? Homework can wait. We'll be having dinner with Mr Khan and his wife. You remember Mr Khan? Ah, there we go. You look positively perfect.'

Observing our reflection in the mirror, I barely manage to suppress a grin. My mother and I couldn't be more opposite if we tried. She's wearing a sleek black dress, tights and pointed pumps. Her hair is a dark chestnut brown like my brother's and combed back into a severe bouffant. There is always something so commanding about her appearance, so ruthless. Perhaps because she's British? I notice her smiling at me and force one back.

'You really do look perfect.' She sighs and I feel my heart lift. All I ever want from my parents is a sign, some small confirmation that I'm doing okay and that they love me unconditionally. I smile back at her once more, only this time it isn't forced.

'Mom, I…'

'Oh, sweetie,' she says glancing down at the breakfast bar poking out the top of my school bag. 'You're not really going to eat that, are you?' Her eyes flick from my bag, to my waist, and then up to meet my own. Then, with a frown, she's off and out the door.

I turn back to the girl in the mirror and I tell her not to cry. I will her to straighten herself out. To forget. My stomach rumbles, aching for that which I mustn't let it have. I have to remain the way she wants me; I have to remain her perfect porcelain doll. The girl in the mirror pleads with me but I look away. I reach down for my bag and zip it shut before slinging it over my shoulder and heading out the door, following in my mother's footsteps.

Outside the air is warm. I stop half-way down the front steps and allow the sunlight to wash over me. Sunlight can be sporadic here in the British South-West, but when it finds its way through the clouds it's dazzling. Of course, it's nothing like the sun I grew so accustomed to back in my old life in California. My family relocated shortly after Jenna's death. Dad is one of the lead researchers at Bio-Chem, an international pharmaceutical company. He said he wanted to be closer to the London branch to oversee the launch of a new experimental medication. My mother wouldn't hear of living in the city though, not with all the smog. A large home somewhere quiet where she could show off her wealth to the lowly locals would suit her nicely. That's when Dad suggested Fortune's Well… I'm not really sure why or how he even knew this poky little town existed.

'Oi, DeeDee, over here!' A voice calls from across the street. It's Vicky Marshall and a few of the other girls from our year. 'Walk with us, babe.' I stroll over to join them, and Vicky loops her arm around mine. 'What d'you think?' She tucks a strand of auburn hair behind her ear and tugs at the oversized hoop earring, 'only twenty quid, but you wouldn't know it, would you?'

'Nice,' I lie.

As we reach the school gates a gang of boys sharing a smoke by the fence call us over. Jared Wheeler and the rugby lot. Suddenly I feel uncomfortable. I notice Jared's gaze travel down my legs and back up to my chest. I pull my blazer around me tighter and clear my throat. Vicky jumps into his arms, interrupting the mental undressing. My boyfriend, Ben Evans, comes over to take my bag and walk me to my first exam. He kisses my cheek and his hand wanders down my back, lower and lower until I swat it away. Jared's beady eyes are back on me now. I feel my cheeks burn. I feel ill.

I have avoided any contact with Jared since Vicky's party last weekend. I'd had a little too much tequila and snuck off into the garden for some air. There I was, leaning forward on the bench, head in hands admiring the dandelions at my feet that seemed to swirl and grow in number the longer I looked. Then I felt the soothing touch of hands on my shoulders. They ran down the front of my top and into my bra, caressing me. Normally I would be far too reserved, but the alcohol made me feel warm and tingly. I felt daring. Adventurous.

I relaxed into his arms, allowing him to take the lead. That's when he spoke softly against my ear and I realised that I was wrong. It wasn't Ben at all, it was that filthy pig Jared Wheeler. He pressed his lips against my neck and held me in place when I tried to wriggle free. One hand clamped on my wrist whilst the other found its way into the waistband of my jeans. I shouted for him to stop but I was far too drunk to fight him off. His fingers scuttled further down across my underwear. Mustering all the strength I could I flung my head back into his face, it caused a cracking noise as it collided with his nose.

'Ow! Bitch!' he cried out, pulling away and spitting a wad of blood onto the grass.

'I said no!' I shot back, refastening my jeans, pulling my shirt back down over me, and crossing my arms over my chest.

Jared observed me for a moment before spitting into the grass once again and smirking.

'Ah well,' he grinned, 'I don't do fat chicks anyway.' Then, just as suddenly as he had appeared, he was gone.

Looking at him now, that same stupid smirk is painted across his face. I avert my gaze as the morning bell rings out and I follow Ben to the examination hall. It's my final exams today before the summer. I'm pretty sure I've done enough revision, but I've still got butterflies.

*

The day is going by so slowly. In fact, I am almost positive the clock has begun to run backwards. I almost don't believe it when the end of school bell chimes out and there I am again on the street outside my home. I climb the stairs to my room and shrug out of my uniform. My stomach rumbles. I reach for the breakfast bar in my bag and wolf it down. I grab another from the secret stash in my underwear drawer. And another. And another.

Now, I'm in the en suite. The usual routine. Hanging over the toilet bowl, throat burning, face wet. But I feel better now. Happier. I rinse my mouth out under the tap and dry my face off against the soft white towel and tiptoe back into my room, knowing that she'll be there—watching me. Judging. Sure enough, there she is, the girl in the mirror. I avert my eyes from hers and grab the blanket from the end of my bed and toss it over her frame until she's suffocated beneath it. I climb into my bed, lift the duvet high above my head, bury my face into the pillows and scream.

3: JJ

I don't fill the jar when Uncle Henry tells me to go to bed. I should, but I don't. Maybe I want to test the theory, see what happens. Tempt fate. Instead, I lay on my bed as the sunlight dwindles outside my window and my crazy mother's pointless jar is on the dresser and I stare at it, daring its emptiness to curse me too.

And I feel a tremor of urges under my skin.

Smash the jar, stomp on the glass, throw it out the window, get rid of it. Because my mother was obviously crazy, *obviously*! She hit my dad in the head with a hammer because she found out he was cheating on her. Normal, sane people don't do things like that. And according to Uncle Henry there was never anything sane about Cora White.

'When she met your dad, she used to tell him stories,' he said to me once when he was in one of his reflective moods, 'and she'd write them all down too, these crazy, dreamlike stories. She had one hell of an imagination, you know that. She made up whole worlds, right? The thing was JJ, your mother didn't know that. She didn't see any of it as make believe. It was all real to her.' He'd reached out and tapped the side of my head, with a troubled look on his face. 'You gotta know the difference up here, right? What's real and what's not? *You* know, don't you JJ?'

I'd said yes, *of course* I knew what was real and what was not.

But looking at the jar now, I wonder how true that statement was. Because my head is full of stories too, and pictures and sometimes it gets so full and so busy in there that it feels like my brain is going to explode. That's why I draw. I've got notebooks and sketchbooks all over the place and they are all full of the stuff in my head.

And sometimes when I'm feeling really intense about something, I can see the things I am supposed to draw. Even before I draw them. And I don't mean I can see them in my head, I mean I can see them on the paper, moving and swirling and forming.

Like now. Uncle Henry is in the lounge with a woman. I think I recognise her voice and if I am right, she is the new waitress at his favourite café in town. She has short brown hair and elfin features, and she is ever so tall and thin. I can hear her moaning as he does things to her in there and I don't like it. I hate it. Sometimes I hate him. I know I ought to be grateful he took me in when there was no one else, but sometimes…

And if I think about Jared Wheeler and those other creeps…if I think about school, if I think about my mother and my dead father, if I think about the black swirling emptiness inside of me…sometimes something happens. The black emptiness appears on the page before me and I feel like I am slipping into a thick trance, a daydream. But I'm just imagining it. I blink hard and look away.

I adjust my position on the bed and lie on my belly, notepad in front of me, pencil behind my ear. I am staring at the empty jar on the dresser when it suddenly starts to fill with what looks like black smoke. Chester starts barking as the waitress gets louder and Uncle Henry throws something at him, and the jar is full of blackness. Maybe it's just a shadow, but the weakness in my bowels suggests otherwise. It's moving in there. Spinning and swirling and maybe if I hadn't clipped the lid down it would spill out, flowing on to the dresser and drifting down to the floor.

I stare at it so long my eyes start to hurt. Then I take the pencil out from behind my ear and I start to draw the jar with the blackness inside of it.

*

The first day of summer.

Morning shattered by the sound of the cockerel screaming and Chester barking. In the next room, my uncle rolls over and falls out of bed. The waitress squeals and then laughs. I get up, get dressed and get into the kitchen before them.

The best way to handle Uncle Henry is to stay out of his way as much as possible. That's not easy when there are just the two of you living in the same small farmhouse and it's not easy when he needs your help around the farm to keep it going. We have to communicate, but I try to keep it to a minimum.

This is why:

Uncle Henry staggers into the kitchen, wiping the sleep from his eyes and yawning as he scratches his stubbled chin.

'What are you looking at?' he grumbles.

I'm not looking at anything, but he's so paranoid, he thinks I am. I mumble 'nothing' and make myself some toast with my back turned to him the whole time.

'You getting out of here later?'

I don't have plans as I don't have any friends, but I don't tell him this, obviously. I just nod my head. 'After my chores, yeah.'

'Good,' he says briskly, putting on the kettle and grabbing two clean mugs from the draining board, 'because the lads are coming over later for a game of cards.'

'Okay.'

I take my toast and walk out of the kitchen. He watches me go and I can feel his bright blue eyes boring into me and I can feel how much he wants to throw an insult at me, but he doesn't, because of the waitress. He doesn't want anyone around here to know he isn't perfect.

Living with Uncle Henry is like living on a minefield. You know the landmines are there, and you do everything you can to avoid them. You step carefully, and precisely and quietly all the time. You do everything right, but you know that one of them will go off eventually.

I try not to think about how much he hates me. Or why.

Because if I do, the darkness starts to fill me. Cold, empty darkness.

Outside, I do my daily chores with the monotonous movements of a well-trained robot. I feed the chickens and ducks, hang out the washing from the machine, feed the cows and muck out their barn. It takes me an hour and then I grab my backpack, fill it with paper and pens and get out of his way.

It's hard being this unwanted, this lonely. It gets boring, it gets stagnant and old. Like everything around me is faded and grey. Sometimes it gets hard to see the green of the trees or the blue of the sky and I think about this as I cross the road and head down the riverside path.

It's still early so I am probably safe. I sit down close to the water on a half rotten log and take out my notepad. At first, my head is just full of Uncle Henry's angry face, the empty jar, dead flowers, and the hammer that killed my dad. So, I draw all of these. Anyone would think I am sat there sketching the river, but I'm not. My page is a scratchy, angry, jumble of faces and eyes, weapons, landmines and broken glass. And then when my head is emptier, the other things creep in. The swirling darkness and the way it moves like something light and gleeful. I draw a boy with his mouth wide open, so wide it has broken his head and the top hangs backwards, touching his shoulders. And I draw the darkness filling him up, spinning like black clouds into his open mouth.

As I draw, my mouth falls open and my tongue creeps out and I swear, I *swear* I can taste the darkness I am drawing. It's both bitter and sour, light and heavy and it wants to get in, I can tell. It wants to consume me. It tastes vile and it tastes good and I am just daydreaming, just playing make believe like Mum used to do when she was a kid. It's not real and if I close my mouth, I won't really swallow it, because it's not real, not real…

'Oh Christ, look who it is,' groans a voice behind me.

I look over my shoulder to see Jared Wheeler, Andrew Hart and Frankie Simpson. What the hell are they doing up this early? Then I see they are dressed in their rugby clothes and covered in mud. They must have had a training session. I sigh and slide my notebook and pen into the backpack, but too late, they saw.

It's Jared who reaches for my bag, using one hand to shove me backwards off the log while he plucks out my notebook, laughing.

'What've we got here?' he sniggers, big greedy smile lighting up his long face. 'Secret diary?'

'It's nothing, give it back.' I scramble to my feet and try to snatch it back, but Jared is quicker and taller, holding it out of my reach.

He flicks through it, turning and shouldering me aside every time I try to grab it.

'It's mine!' I hiss, getting angrier. 'Give it back!'

One of the others kicks my legs out from under me and I hit the ground, scraping my chin, but I jump back up, not wanting to give them any leverage.

'Oh my God, you gotta see this,' squeals Jared, shoving me away again.

This time I land on my arse, and now all three of them are crowded around my notebook and they are laughing and pointing at my sketches and laughing and pointing at me. And I know it can't be true, can't be real, but I can see that black mist again, and it's in thick plumes creeping around their ankles.

It must be a daydream, a trick of the light. It's dark down here alongside the river, under the trees and there are shadows and variations of light and shade. They don't seem to notice either, they don't see what I see - black mist circling their legs, so dark now I cannot see their feet.

I let out a loud bellow of utter rage and fear and throw myself at them.

4: Darcie

It's morning once again, only this time I am not met with the shrill cry of my mother. With school no longer in session, things have gone back to normal and she has forgotten I exist. *Good.* Rubbing the sleep from my eyes I slip into a pair of track shorts and the nearest hoodie I can find, pull my hair back into my signature ponytail, and pop-in my headphones. Downstairs Jeremy is watching cartoons and bouncing up and down on the couch in the den with his best friend, Chris. *Isn't fourteen a little too old for Sponge Bob?* I wonder as I pull on my running shoes. My mother must be out at the market with Julia, that's the only reason Jeremy would be brave enough to use the furniture as a trampoline. I hear a noise from the living room.

'Morning, Dad.'

'If you could just get them to double-check the levels. They might need resetting.'

'Dad?'

'Perfect, thank you so much, Angelique. Yes, yes, I'll be back in the office soon.'

'I'm just heading out to meet Vicky.'

'Oh, and did you manage to email the report?'

'We're gonna go smoke weed and have sex, lots and lots of sex. Maybe even with each other.'

'Hold on two seconds, Angie. Okay pumpkin, I'm working right now.' He flashes me a smile and places the phone back to his ear. It's strange how he can look so much like Aunt Jenna with his perfect blonde hair and blue eyes but be completely unlike her in so many other ways. Everything with Dad is work, work, work.

I hover in the doorway and wait for him to process what I just said but there is absolutely no reaction. He is straight back to talking about stock levels and reports. I slip out the front door unnoticed and I'm delighted to see the sun once more. With a deep breath I begin a slow jog up the road towards town. My body aches a little, but I ignore it, losing myself in the words of *To All of You* by Syd Matters as they flood into my ears.

In my pocket my phone rumbles, I tug out my headphones and swipe open the screen: *One new message from Vicky Marshall.* It's a photo of my back. I turn and see her skipping up the street behind me.

'Mornin' sleepy-head,' she mocks. 'Want one?'

I shake my head at the cigarette packet clamped between her hot pink nails. I'm not feeling it. Not today.

'Ah, suit yourself.' She lifts one to her lips and struggles to light it. 'You know what, DeeDee?' she mumbles as she continues to wrestle with the lighter. 'You've been a real downer lately. Everyone's been saying it. Not just me.'

I stay quiet.

'Do they have Benson 'n' Hedges in America?' she asks, removing the cigarette from her mouth and admiring it. A plume of smoke wafts in my direction. I cough and look away.

'I don't know…'

'Hm.' She shrugs at me and takes another puff. A few wisps of white ash float up into her hair.

'I thought we were meeting in town?'

'Change of plans, babe. We're meeting the lads down at Swimmo's.'

I grimace. *Swimmo's* was the name of a large portion of the river, which was once an outdoor swimming pool during wartime. An outbreak of polio decades ago had caused it to shut down. Now all that remained were a few crumbling walls at the edges of the grass verge. Jared and his goons like to go there when the weather is hot and dare each other to do summersaults off the edge. My mind turns to Jared Wheeler posing in his swim shorts and I can't help but frown.

'Something wrong?'

'No.'

I wait for her to follow up, to see the concern in my eyes and press for answers but she doesn't. Nobody ever does. I don't mean to sound so depressing, honestly, I don't, but I am just a token to them. A novelty. The shiny new rich girl all the way from California. They don't really care what goes on in my mind, or even how I'm feeling. They just want me looking my best so that they can too. That's why Vicky chose me for her circle. That's why my parents want me and Jeremy to attend their business dinners. Of course, Jeremy can't see that yet though. He just sits there and smiles and hides his Brussels sprouts under his perfectly folded napkin.

*

The presence of Jared Wheeler is unmistakable as we make our way along the winding river path. There is a heavy stench of Lynx deodorant in the air and around the next bend I can hear his stupid laugh.

'Kill him Jared!'

'Knock his fuckin' block off!'

I can see them now, Andrew Hart and Frankie Simpson. They are bouncing around like apes. Howling with laughter. On the ground before them Jared is knelt with someone in a headlock. All I can see is a thatch of blonde hair.-

'Simps!' Vicky is oblivious to the boy on the ground and goes running over to Frankie. 'You were supposed to call Alice back last night.' She shoves him.

Seriously? Is nobody going to say anything here?

I look down at the boy on the ground. His face is turning purple, Jared's bulky arm is wrapped around his throat like a python. I look at the others. They are chatting now. Laughing. Sharing memes on their phones. The boy on the ground makes a sound. Jared laughs then spits on him.

'Stupid little queer.'

I don't know what I'm thinking but I pick up a rock at my feet. I rush forward and smack him in the back of the head with it so hard it hurts my hand. Vicky is shouting at me now.

'Babe, what the fuck!?'

I raise the rock again. Jared turns his face towards me and laughs. The boy is scratching at his arm. I see Jared's smug grin. I see his lips against my ear. I see his hands slipping into my jeans. I see red.

Thwack. The rock collides against the side of his cheek. He pushes the boy into the dirt and charges me, but Vicky stands in the way.

'Hey, Wheeler calm down man,' says Frankie.

'Yeah, just chill mate,' adds Andrew.

Jared just stands there, red-faced from blood and anger. His shoulders moving up and down as he huffs in and out.

'Oh, baby you're gonna need stitches in that,' says Vicky. She licks her thumbs and rubs it against the gash on his cheek and shoots me a look. I know that look. It means '*what the fuck is wrong with you!?*' I stay silent. The rock rolls from my fingers and lands with a thud.

The group begin moving off and I turn my attention once more to the boy on the ground. His fists are dug into the grass and he's shaking. I reach down, pick up his glasses and hand them back to him. He seems a little nervous at first, but he reaches out and takes them.

Suddenly, I see it - next to him in the grass is a thick black mist. That stupid prick Jared Wheeler must have chucked down a smoke. Did he not watch the news? True, it's not as if we live out in the middle of the Australian bush but wildfires could still happen here in the small town of Fortune's Well. I gasp and stomp on the ground. I keep stomping but the mist continues to grow. It swirls around my ankle and I watch in confusion as it begins to dissipate and disappear into the dirt below. I check the grass for a stray cigarette end to make sense of what I am seeing but there isn't one.

The boy looks up at me, then he follows my eyeline to the ground. He looks up at my face once more, open-mouthed. I think he is going to say something, but he doesn't.

'Sorry about your book,' I finally manage, pointing at the sketch pad in front of him that has been stomped into the mud.

He scurries towards it but still doesn't respond.

'Okay then…' I say with a grin, and as I turn to leave, the rock by my feet catches my eye. In my head I see the dumb smirk leaving Jared's face as I hit him with it only moments before. I reach into my pocket and place my headphones back into my ears, hit play on my phone, break into a jog and smile.

5: JJ

I stay by the river after they leave. The mist has gone but I want it to come back. I stare at the ground, at the river, at my ruined notebook, *willing* it. But nothing happens. And I keep thinking about that girl, I think her name is Darcie - why did she stamp on the ground like that? Did she see it too?

Eventually, I crawl over to my bag and stuff the wrecked book back inside. I zip it up, stagger to my feet and brush down my clothes. My glasses are a bit bent, so the world looks lop-sided when I put them back on. I rub my neck, sigh heavily and start to trudge home.

When I reach the farmyard, Uncle Henry is there changing a tyre on his Land Rover. When he sees the state of me, he throws down his cigarette, grabs my arm and marches me towards the barn.

'Fucks sake, JJ, in there, *now*!'

I yank my arm free and face him. 'What for? What's the point?'

He steps back and looks me up and down like I am a complete mystery to him. 'The point is I'm sick of you coming home like this; don't you want to stand up for yourself?'

I gesture angrily at the barn. 'It doesn't matter, it doesn't help when there's three of them and one of me!'

Uncle Henry rolls his eyes, holds my shoulder, and steers me firmly into the barn. 'Oh, boo hoo, poor JJ,' he says, snatching up the boxing gloves from the stack of straw bales behind him. 'You just want to give up, is that it?'

I want to kill them.

I let him tie the gloves on to my hands and I say nothing as he urges me to take up my position at the punchbag. I just shake my head and grit my teeth. He holds up my hands, forces them into the correct place. He stills the punchbag and looks at me.

'You only need to beat one of them,' he says, 'just one. The other's back down. You just need to beat the ringleader.'

'You should've let me keep the knife then.'

'Shut up,' he growls. 'Right hook.'

I punch the bag. Hard. I picture Jared Wheeler's face on it and punch it again.

'That's it,' Uncle Henry holds the bag and that makes me want to punch it even harder. I want him to feel it too - all the solid blackness inside of me. I want him to know how it feels to carry that around. 'C'mon, put your shoulders into it, move around a bit like I showed you. C'mon, not like a little pussy JJ, like a man! Show me!'

It doesn't matter how hard I hit it. It doesn't matter how far back Uncle Henry gets shoved as he hangs on to the bag. It doesn't matter how much he yells at me or tells me how much of a little pussy I am. It doesn't matter. *Nothing* matters.

I punch it until we are both sweating and panting. I punch it until he tells me to stop and even then, I keep going, throwing my fists, and seeing Jared's face. I punch his face until it becomes misty and starts to dissipate.

Uncle Henry pulls me away from the bag and then lights a cigarette. 'Not too shabby,' he says as he starts to walk away. 'Keep that up and you'll beat them one day.'

He's almost out of the door when I ask him. 'Did my dad box? Did my dad box like you Uncle Henry?'

He pauses but doesn't answer. I stare at his back, at his broad shoulders and his blue and black checked shirt and the way the farm muscles fill every inch of it, and from

25

behind, he looks so much like my dad that it crushes my windpipe and I'm unable to breathe. My lips tremble with tears I can't cry and his shoulders drop and I desperately want him to say something to me, something gentle and kind, something about my dad and how proud of me he would be. Something. Anything.

But then he straightens up and his muscles tighten and he throws the insult over his shoulder because of course he can't even be bothered to look at me: 'Your dad was a man, JJ, not a weirdo pussy like you, getting your arse whipped every day. He didn't have to come in here and box.'

That's it. That's what I get. Uncle Henry keeps walking but turns around to point his cigarette at me. 'Don't forget you're out of here later! Go get cleaned up and find some place to go.'

That's how it is.

*

I walk along the river path, one small notebook stuffed in the back pocket of my jeans, alongside a pencil. Another pencil behind my ear. I kick along, and I am full of hate, full of disgust, full of self-loathing, so full up I want to tip back my head and scream at the sky. But I don't. Instead I let my head fill with all the things I should draw; they come to life there first, sketched in blood and pain and emptiness.

I think about my mother's jar and how I should stop being a wuss and just smash it or fill it again. Fill it with what? What makes me happy? What makes me smile? And I can't find anything. Not one single thing. Thinking about my mother is too painful. It makes me want to sink my fingernails into my flesh and dig down to the bone. I see her once a month if I am lucky, but Uncle Henry doesn't like it. He says each time I come back even weirder and it's his job to make sure I don't turn out like her.

At the end of the river walk, I start to climb the steep hill that will lead me into town. I am being drawn to something, but I don't know what. It's like my notebook is quivering and my pencil is trembling with want and need. At the top of the hill is the big roundabout and from there I head down the road known as 'the walks.' It's lined with trees and I stop at almost every one, pulling out my notebook to sketch and scribble.

I am aware of how strange I must look; how much people must want to laugh at and ridicule me. The weird boy with the dead dad and the crazy mum. No wonder no one gives me the time of day. They are scared of me - afraid I'll taint them with my madness.

I go through the gates and enter the park. The bandstand takes centre place and it's empty, so I head there to kill some time. I lean over the notebook and start to draw. It's like the pencil takes over, leading me this way and then that. It dances across the page, creating lines and forms and faces. I draw the punchbag and I draw Jared and I draw Uncle Henry and my mother and they are all dancing around the bandstand, holding hands, their mouths thrown open in crazy laughter.

Time flies when you are lost and alone. Before I know it, the sun is slipping down behind the trees, casting a golden light across the grass. Teenagers are slipping into the park now, in pairs and in groups. From the bandstand, I am hidden, and I can hear their soft laughter, their murmuring desires, and budding plans. I hunch over my knees, pencil poised on soft paper. I feel so alone there, so separate, so *empty* that it physically hurts, and I honestly don't know what to do with this much pain.

Then I hear their voices. The same crowd from this morning - Jared and his friends, and the girls. They are under the trees and I can smell their cigarettes and hear the hiss of their cans opening. The girls are laughing, and it makes me ache inside to hear something so carefree, so full of life.

They don't know I am here and it must stay that way or I'll get into another fight and I'll lose again and Uncle Henry will despise me even more. Unless...

I think about what he said. About only having to beat one, the ringleader. Of course, he was right, he's *always* right. And if it were possible...if I could beat Jared somehow, get him alone or challenge him to a fair fight... My mind tumbles with the possibilities and suddenly the black smoke is back.

I pull back when I see it. I press myself against the wooden railings and close my mouth, suddenly terrified that it wants to seep inside of me. It's just a tendril at first, snaking around my feet, teasingly. I tell myself it can't be real...I can't be seeing this, but it's there, and it's faster now, coiling around my calves. I brush at it but my fingers go right through it and come away cold.

I scramble to my feet and try to kick it away in a panic, but it won't go, it won't even dissipate or fade, and if anything, it's getting thicker.

'Shit!' I bite back a scream and that's when Jared Wheeler sees me.

6: Darcie

I really don't want to go to the park.

Since the events earlier in the day, where I bashed Jared Wheeler's face in with the rock, I could tell that my already miserable life was about to get a whole lot worse—especially with storm Vicky raging on the horizon. After the field, we didn't say a word. I continued my jog, right out to the edges of town and up to the lumpy hill which once supported a proud stone castle. Now though, all that is left is a discarded shell. A husk. Reminding me of myself.

I'd jogged so hard my feet began to throb with every pound against the pavement. But I didn't care. All I wanted to do was keep running until the town and all those in it were a distant memory.

Something pulled me back though. I'd like to say it was a sense of responsibility for people like that boy at the river, people that needed my help from assholes like Jared Wheeler. But really, I think it was fear. Fear of leaving. Fear of the unknown. Fear of not being missed at all. At least at home there was some hope, however slight, that perhaps one day things would change.

Coming back, however, soon felt like a mistake.

Right now, I'm crouched on the floor in the en suite with my knees under my chin. From the floor below, I can hear the shouts of Ben and Jeremy. They're playing video games whilst I 'finish my math homework.' I think deep down Ben knows me well enough to know I've already completed it, but at least it buys me a little more time to prepare for the inevitable. Tonight, our friends, if I can still call them that, have all arranged to meet for drinks at the park in the centre of town. As much as I insist, 'I don't want to go', Ben won't take no for an answer. Initially, I thought this was some noble, romantic gesture.

'Come on, Darcie, I want to take you out for the evening and have fun. I want to show you off to the world. Who cares what you've done? I support you.' It didn't take me long to realise that it's simply because it will be, quote, *'embarrassing'* for him if I don't show up, when all the other girlfriends are going. So that's it. It's all about his ego.

Next to me my phone vibrates against the tiled flooring. It's Ben. *Why is it when I want to be invisible I can't?* I wrap my fingers around the basin and haul my frame up from the floor. It feels lighter than it did before I entered the en suite. I walk through my bedroom with a sigh, this time not caring to look and see if the girl in the mirror is watching me, and stomp down the stairs. *Thump. Thump. Thump.* Ben is already waiting at the bottom, arms folded. He doesn't say anything about the wetness of my face or seem to have any concern about the way I wobble slightly, and clasp hold of the banister for support. Instead, he just glances at the Armani watch on his wrist and sulks.

'We're gonna be late.'

'You could have gone without me.'

Silence.

A look.

I pull on my jacket.

The walk to the park should only take twenty-minutes tops, but we've already been walking for over thirty. Ben says I'm dawdling. He's right. But fuck him. I don't even want to go to the stupid park anyway. I feel bad for thinking that. The park itself isn't bad… I've spent plenty of lazy hours here with Vicky gossiping by the old fountain and trying to climb the edges of the gigantic clock. That clock seems smaller now somehow.

The gates are up ahead, my pulse quickens. I feel it throbbing in my neck. Ben doesn't understand why I did what I did to Jared Wheeler, and this angers me. Why am I the only one that sees the way our group is treating other people is wrong? He says I did it for attention. That I'm stupid. When I go quiet, he reaches for my ass and tries to pull me closer, as if that is going to change anything. I've started to realise that Ben has been under Jared's spell for far too long.

When I open the gates, I feel my stomach hit the concrete. Vicky is already here and she's lying on the grassy mounds between the flower beds, laughing with the other girls. I spot Gemma Hallett a mile away. *So, she's my replacement this evening?* I feel bad for her. Gemma is a nice girl, sweet, polite, and popular with everyone. I imagine Vicky invited her solely to hurt me. Sure enough, I am right. Vicky has spotted us coming down the winding path and is immediately pulling Gemma tighter and whispering against her ear. They face me and giggle before Rachel Edgar and Becky Grey wave me over.

I turn to my right, intending to take hold of Ben's hand and take him over with me, but he's already over by the boys. They're kicking around a football and knocking back cans of beer. Frankie throws one to Ben and he catches it with a smirk, which soon leaves his face when he cracks it open and an eruption of froth spills out on his jeans. Becky thrusts a pack of sour sweets at me. I place my hand inside and hesitate as I notice Jared staring me down.

'I don't do fat chicks.'

I drop the handful of sugar back into the pack with a grimace and pass them across to Rachel. She smiles at me and snatches them away so greedily that I'm afraid if I move any slower, she'd snatch my fingers off too. I dust my hands off against my jeans and dare to peer up at Vicky. She notes my attempt and her eyes immediately dart the other way. Although the other girls are chattering away and laughing, there is a definite tension. It is almost as if I could put a pin up to the air and it would burst like a balloon. A huge balloon full of shit. Vicky clears her throat and I know what's coming, but right when she's about to say something catty a noise from across the way catches my attention.

It's the boy from the river. He's on the bandstand looking back at us like a rabbit in the headlights and for a moment the world is still. Almost instinctively my fingers dig into the grass below me as I wait for Jared to go marching across the path to grab him by the neck again and force his face into the dirt. If he does, I don't know how I'll react.

I'll probably lose it entirely and it will be the end for me with my friends. Full on social suicide. But I can't take the bullying any longer, I can't take the standing back and staying quiet. The denying of involvement when questioned by teachers, the catty remarks or tearing down other girls because of the size of their chests. I can't take Jared and Vicky and all this popular kid bullshit. I am sick of being a puppet. A prop. Sick of it all.

Vicky is still babbling away in my ear, so self-absorbed as usual that she hasn't even noticed the boy. Across the way Jared moves and I flinch. But then he does something unexpected. He places both hands into his pockets and starts strolling off into the shady area in the far corner of the park. Vicky climbs to her feet and calls after him.

'Babe, where you goin'?'

'To take a leak,' Jared spits back. He's stalking towards the run-down public toilets and doesn't bother to look back at us, not once. I feel my grip on the grass relax. *Phew.* The girls continue to chat amongst themselves and every time their focus falls on me, Vicky is sure to interrupt and abruptly change the subject. I smile along, playing my part and tolerating it. *One more evening can't hurt, can it? Not when I know the role so well.*

Suddenly, I notice something is very wrong. The boy from the river is no longer in sight. I look for him underneath the trees and over by the fountain, but he's gone. Now I spot him. He's stomping past the bowls green in the direction of the toilets with a look of sheer determination on his face. *This can't be good.* I climb to my feet, without bothering to excuse myself and begin moving off in his direction.

'Erm, where d'you think you're goin'?'

Vicky is on her feet now too, red-faced and arms folded. Before I can answer she steps over the other girls, grabs hold of my arm and pulls me off towards a neighbouring flower bed.

'I've let it slide for long enough now, DeeDee, but you need to stop!'

'Stop what?'

She rolls her eyes at me as I stare coolly back, confused.

'Going after my boyfriend. I know that's why you lost it earlier. I heard about how you couldn't keep your hands off him at my party.' I'm speechless, and I feel sick. I feel it bubbling up and burning inside of me. 'See, you're not even denying it.'

She's smirking at me now. That same smirk that Jared does. And Ben. And all these other sheep. I wrench her grip from my arm and shove her away.

'You know what Vicky, fuck you!'

The heads of the other girls snap up in unison. They are staring at us like little field mice, too scared to come out from cover for fear of being eaten. Vicky makes a noise with her tongue and walks back over to take her place amongst them. 'Whatever.'

Remembering why I got up in the first place I hurriedly make my way towards the toilets. They are in a small building situated behind a jungle of weeds. The council are in the process of building a new block over the other side of the park where the fancy new outdoor gym set is. I hover outside for a moment, wringing my hands and taking a deep breath before I finally have the courage to enter the men's unit. Everything inside is dark and silent. It reeks of mould and urine. I pull the sleeves of my jacket down over my hands and feel my way around the wall, stumbling along the row of sinks and stalls, all the way to the large troth at the end. *That's weird. They're not here.*

I fumble around the damp floor, my shoes sliding against the dead leaves and toilet roll, and head back the way I came, but as I pass the first stall a hand wraps into my hair and tugs my neck back with such force, I fear it might snap. There's a hand on my throat now too. I can't breathe. I kick out my feet and try to make a sound but it's no use. I know that smell. I try to angle my face towards one of the mirrors above the sinks. Sure enough, it's the devil himself, Jared Wheeler. I struggle and he places his lips to my ear.

'Not so tough now are we, slut?'

I want to break free with every inch of my being. I want to cry out for help. But I feel far too weak to fight. *Maybe I did take it too far earlier, back home in the en suite.* My sides ache at the thought. I try to fling my head back into him like I had at the party but it's no use. His grip is far too strong. He presses me forward so that the side of my face is stuck against the filthy mirror. I feel him tugging at the back of my jeans and pulling down his own. He wraps my ponytail tighter around his hand and I see that smug grin in the reflection. He sticks out his tongue and licks at the scab on his cheek.

'It's payback time, bitch.'

I'm screaming, I swear I'm screaming, but no noise is coming out. I close my eyes.

Crack!

I open them and to my surprise there he is, the boy from the river. He's emerged from one of the stalls behind us with his fists held high in front of his face. For a moment I think I am imagining him, until he steps forward and delivers another hard blow to Jared's face. And another. And another. Around his arms a thick mist begins to spill out and flood the air, at first like a fog or a haze and then thicker, darker, until all I see is black. He swings again, but Jared blocks him with his forearm and delivers a punch right back. It collides with the boy's chest hard but he isn't fazed. He just keeps swinging. Wild, aggressive. He delivers one final punch square against Jared's face. The force causes him to stagger backwards and with his jeans still down by his ankles he stumbles, his head colliding against one of the sinks with a deafening crack.

A commotion from outside steals my focus, one of the boys must have come looking for Jared, and from the small window I see the glare of torchlight and hear the familiar jingle of keys. The groundskeeper.

'What the bloody hell's going on here?' I hear him ask, followed by muffled voices and the rattle of beer cans.

The boy from the river grabs my arm and I'm shocked by how soft his touch is. He waits for some sign from me first that it's okay before pulling me out the door. We hunch down through the weeds and off into the abandoned club house by the bowls green. The boy smashes the window and wrenches open the door and together we hide inside. I hear a scream. It's Vicky. They must have found Jared. I wonder if he's dead, and part of me hopes he is because if not, soon enough, we will be. I turn to face the boy as we huddle below the window frame. I haven't said a word since Jared grabbed me back in the bathroom but, somehow, I know I am safe with him. For a moment it occurs to me just how poetic this scenario is, I saved him earlier at the river and now he's saved me. I rest my head against his shoulder and sigh.

7: JJ

This can't be happening…

It's like a dream and it all happened so fast that I know I will be lying awake in bed all night trying to piece it back together again. Trying to relive it… I'm shaking hard. My eyes feel too wide and my skin too hot and when I look down at my fists, I swear I can still see the black swirls drifting around them.

Darcie is resting her head on my shoulder and suddenly that helps - suddenly her doing that gives me exactly what I need to think clearly. Jared was hurting her. He was going to attack her.

So, it's not just me…

She's shaking too. She must be in shock. I lift my arm slowly and stiffly and wrap it around her shoulder. The torchlight bounces around outside for a few more moments and then starts to drift away. The groundskeeper might be heading off, but Jared and his friends are all still out there.

'I think we need to get out of here,' I whisper. She lifts her head and stares at me, biting her lip, trying not to cry and I nod at her. 'Darcie, right?'

She nods again. 'And you're-'

'JJ.'

She smiles and wipes a stray hair from her face. 'I think you just saved my life, JJ.'

'Nah.' I glance away before straightening up to check the window. 'We gotta go.'

She gets to her feet nodding and I open the door slowly and glance out before committing to movement. I start to move when she stops me, grabbing my arm.

'What was that stuff?' she hisses, and in the darkness, I can see the whites of her eyes, the fear in them. I stare back at her and I want to tell her I don't know, I didn't see any stuff, but I can tell that she is not kidding.

'I don't know what you mean,' I reply softly.

She nods as if this is enough for her and she follows me out of the building. For a moment, I'm lost. I don't know what to do. I just beat Jared up. The other kids are still around. The black mist…it did something to me. It was like it was there when I needed it, but that can't be possible, can it? Does all this mean Uncle Henry was right? I'm as crazy as my mother? I want Darcie to ask me again, to tell me what she saw so that I know I'm not losing my mind but not yet. We have to get out of here first.

*

It's getting dark by the time we arrive back at the farm. The sun is lower now and Uncle Henry's fields are lit up with pink and gold. He's there in the yard, still tinkering with the rusty old Land Rover and laughing with his mates. There are two of them sprawled in rickety deck chairs with beers on the go. Friends he's had for years; friends who knew my dad.

I feel shaky as we come through the gate. It's everything hitting me at once: the smoke, what it means, what I did to Jared, Darcie and a warm feeling in my belly as Uncle Henry looks up, clocks us and grins.

He drinks his beer and looks Darcie up and down. I'm suddenly horribly aware of how attractive she is…

'Who's this then, JJ?'

'Darcie,' I mumble and start to shift towards the house.

Uncle Henry raises his eyebrows, gives her a charming little bow, and then grins wildly at his friends who are all staring at us.

'Nice to meet you,' Darcie smiles, looking incredibly at ease, almost as if she is playing a part.

'We were just gonna get a drink…' I dare a look at Uncle Henry, who frowns back at me and then slings an arm around my neck.

'Oh sure, you go on. Any trouble tonight?'

He means Jared. I wince slightly but look into his eyes and nod firmly. 'Yeah, but I did what you said. I sorted it. For good.'

Uncle Henry winks at me. He slaps my back and as he turns back to his friends he says, 'that's my boy.'

I'm floating… I can barely walk. I just blink and blink and somehow put one foot in front of the other and lead Darcie into the house.

That's my boy, that's my boy…

My dad used to say that to me. Uncle Henry *never* says things like that. *That's my boy…*

I offer Darcie a Coke and she nods, forcing a smile now, those deep blue eyes starting to shine with tears. Uncle Henry and his friends sound rowdy outside, so I gesture upstairs and lead her up to my room. I don't know what I'm doing. I don't have friends. I don't hang out with girls, let alone ones as pretty and popular as Darcie.

She looks around my room, frowning slightly before she perches on the edge of my unmade bed. I have a sudden inexplicable fear that I've left dirty underwear on the floor or something. My mouth has gone terribly dry and I don't seem to know what to do with my face anymore.

Darcie suddenly leans over her knees and drops her head into her hands. 'Oh shit, oh shit, oh *shit*,' she mumbles and her breath hitches as if she is trying not to sob.

I just stand there holding the drinks and not knowing what the hell to do or say. There is a strange girl in my room, my uncle was nice to me and the black mist I thought was just in my head helped me beat the shit out of Jared Wheeler. I mean, there just aren't any words…

I open my mouth, but nothing comes out.

'Oh shit,' she sniffs, her eyes screwed up behind her hands. 'What're we gonna do?'

'Do you wanna call your parents?' I say, finally putting the drinks down on my dresser next to my mum's jar. It's a stupid thing to say but I don't have anything else. I am still trying to work out how the hell my day ended up with Darcie Duffield in my bedroom and Uncle Henry calling me his boy.

'No,' she shakes her head, drops her hands, and looks at me. 'Do you think he's really hurt? What the hell even happened back there?'

I sit down beside her, not too close, and clasp my hands between my knees. 'I don't know.'

'Do you think he's okay?' She's staring at me, wanting answers and I'm suddenly terrified. Okay, I saved her, I got her away from that creep, but did I go too far? Jared wasn't exactly fighting back by the time we left. She's looking at me in a way that reminds me horribly of how Uncle Henry looks at me. Like I've lost the plot just like Mum, or I'm about to.

I run a hand back through my hair. 'I don't really care,' I say, because why not? I *don't* care about Jared Wheeler. I don't care if he's hurt after the shit he's been giving me lately. Maybe I should care, maybe I should be scared like

40

she is, but I'm not, and if that freaks her out, fine. She can leave.

'What?' she says.

I shrug. 'I hate the guy. He's a shit. He deserved it and if I hadn't stepped in, you'd be the one hurt right now.' I don't look at her. I can't. I just stare ahead.

'But...' Darcie starts and then trails off, looking lost. She wipes her eyes on the sleeves of her hoodie and then folds her arms over her chest.

'I bet he's fine,' I mutter. 'Guys like him always are.'

Darcie looks at me then. Really looks at me. 'Down at the river this morning,' she says, 'I thought I saw this black mist, or smoke or something. I thought someone had started a fire with a cigarette end but...' she pauses again, swallowing hard. I finally meet her eye and although shiny with tears, they are bright and fierce.

We stare at each other with something, some truth, floating between us, just words in the air waiting to be spoken, waiting to be given weight and meaning. And I think if either of us speak them, it will make them real, make them true and I suppose for that long, heavy moment neither of us wants to do that. We could just brush it off I think, pretend it didn't happen, pretend it was just a fight, nothing else.

She bites her lip, and I can tell she is fighting with it too, whether to say the words or just assume she imagined it. I think, maybe she wants me to say it, tell her what she saw was real both times and that it comes from me, from the weird boy JJ Carson, the one whose mother is locked up for murder.

And it all feels too much. Never mind our shared experience, never mind rescuing her from Jared, never mind making Uncle Henry smile at me like I was a human for once. What if she thinks I'm crazy, or worse, dangerous? What if she's right and Jared really is hurt badly? What if they're all out there now looking for me?

Shit. Shit. Shit.

I can't do it.

I get up and pull out my phone. 'I don't know what you're talking about,' I say, churlishly. 'I better call you a taxi. It's getting dark.'

8: Darcie

'93 Elizabeth Avenue, please.'

As I climb into the warmth of the back seat I glance back over my shoulder at my new partner in crime. I smile, but he averts his eyes, hands firmly in his pockets. By the front door the older men are knocking back the final dregs of beer. The one he calls Uncle Henry is leaning against the wall with his arms folded across his chest. He nods at me and I raise my hand and wave back awkwardly. Before I have a chance to say anything more to JJ, he is closing the door on me. I wonder if perhaps it was something I said… something about the way I acted that caused him to feel so uncomfortable. Does he perhaps blame me for what happened tonight? *I hope not.* It feels great to finally meet someone else in this town that seems to be on the same page as me. I don't want to lose him. Not now.

As the car rumbles down the dark country road towards the bright lights of town I feel my stomach begin to ache. We reach a set of traffic lights by the pub along the river and for a moment I consider wrenching open the door and running off into the fields. Running until I can't run any longer. Running back to the farm. Back to JJ.

JJ Carson…

The more I think about him, the faster the memories flood my mind. Although I've never spoken to him before this morning, I know enough about him to realise he doesn't have any friends at school. I wish I'd stopped the hazing sooner, but I was too caught up in the Wheeler-Marshall bubble to say anything. At least that's what I tell myself as I feel the ache in my stomach worsen. *Did he recognise me?* He must have thought I was a complete and utter bitch for not mentioning anything sooner.

I remember speaking to his uncle once before though. Henry Carson. He helped my mother when her car broke down on the road into town. I recall her swooning over his muscular arms. It was one of the only times I had seen my mother flustered and not her usual stick-in-the-mud self. And again, a year or so later, Vicky had pointed him out at the Christmas Carnival. He was dressed from head to toe in a Santa suit and she made some comment about being a very bad girl all year. She must have thought she was irresistible, but I am pretty sure he saw nothing but a petulant child.

Somewhere, wriggling in the back of my mind a memory is beginning to weave its way to the forefront. It was something Vicky told me. Something about Henry Carson's brother being murdered by his own wife, and how he had no choice but to take in their kid. *'Mum says the good ones always have baggage.'* Of course, I'd heard the rumours but the thing about small towns is you never really know what to believe. Gossip spreads like wildfire, and it only takes one small Marshall shaped match to start it off.

I wonder where his mother is. I'm almost certain I'd heard she got banged up in some sort of mental hospital, but the other kids swore blind she had offed herself. And what was with that strange mist I saw swirling around him? It was dark in the bathroom, but I know what I saw. I'm positive it was the same fog-like smoke I saw billowing around the ground down by the river.

I tried to ask him about it back in the club house. Of course, he made out he had no idea what I was talking about, but I know he knows I saw it. I played it cool though, I'm used to keeping my mouth shut and not asking any questions.

It's obvious he doesn't trust me enough to discuss it and why would he? I'm just another rich girl from town. He has absolutely no reason to believe I'm anything more or less than that. Unless of course you count that epic rock to Jared's face incident. I even shocked myself with that one. I tried mentioning it again in his room, thinking that maybe in the safety of his own space he might open up to me but something in him changed. His eyes grew dark and that's when I knew the window of opportunity had slammed shut. So now here I sit, just as alone as ever, but now, at least, with the knowledge that there is someone out there who is just as fucked up as me.

*

Finally, it's morning. I spent the entire night tossing and turning. Reliving that awful experience in the toilet block. Sometimes JJ would come and rescue me as he had done in real life, but other times…

My parents haven't even noticed me; they are far too involved in their morning rituals. In the den Jeremy is glued to the television. I'm surprised by how early he is up before I realise that today is football. I slip on my shoes, saying a silent 'thank you' to Julia for cleaning off the mud, and break out into the early morning air. This morning, like most mornings, I manage to avoid breakfast. Only today it isn't because of the way I feel about myself. It's because for once my mind is otherwise occupied. In my head a swarm of questions about JJ Carson are buzzing around like bees. I need answers. I need to find out more about him, to better understand his story so he knows that he can trust me.

I'm on the bus now and once again my stomach is aching, only this time with excitement. I hop off in town and rush down the cobbled street and up the stone steps of the library. I push open the heavy oak doors and feel immediately transported. There is something so magical about this place… The smell, the calming sound of pages turning as knowledge is being greedily devoured. Of course, I could never admit that to my *friends*. They'd think I'd lost the plot. I laugh. As if it makes any difference now. I scurry to the back wall where the collection of old newspapers are stored. You're supposed to ask an assistant for permission but seeing as I'm a Duffield, my parents' generous donations to the town means I can just breeze right through.

Maybe I am crazy, I tell myself as I begin riffling through a wodge of files. There has to be something in here about the Carson family—there just has to be. It seems like an age but finally I find the articles I am looking for. I lift out the first one and unfold it onto the small metal desk next to me. On the front is the image of a dejected looking woman. Dark circles hide her eyes, and there are deep creases in her skin, but it is clear to see that she was once very beautiful. Her hair falls down around her in a frantic mess. Above her head in heavy block capitals are the words '*HAMMER HEAD HORROR.*' I grimace as I scrape the chair out from under the desk and sit down to read.

Local family in mourning as loved one is murdered in cold blood by doting wife, Cora Carson. It is believed that Mr Carson returned home from work to find his wife absolutely hysterical. Neighbours reported that Mrs Carson (AKA Ms White) had been in an erratic state for a number of days prior to the murder, and that several noise complaints had been made to the authorities. When Mr Carson

46

attempted to calm his wife from the episode, he was struck not once, but forty-seven times against the base of the skull with a hammer from his own toolkit. Cora Carson's legal representation is pleading diminished responsibly by claiming Mrs Carson was mentally unstable at the time of the crime. Carson's death and his wife's arrest leave young son, JJ Carson, practically orphaned. It is unknown at this time if the child will enter the system or be adopted by local relatives. Though evidence of Mrs Carson's poor mental health on the evening of the murder is uncontested, it is unknown whether there are any heredity issues.

I'm speechless. I feel absolutely terrible for JJ. What an awful thing for him to have to go through at such a young age… or at any age really. To lose both his mother and father like that. He probably feels entirely alone in the world.

I feel silly for thinking this, but despite having both my parents alive and well, I can relate. I cast my eyes back over the article and in my mind's eye I see his father's skull being bashed over and over until there is nothing left but a bloody pulp.

Now I'm thinking of Aunt Jenna. I remember how my parents told me that her truck flipped over the edge of the canyon on her way back from a vacation with friends. How it rolled down into the valley. I can see Jenna's smiling face being thrashed and banged against the steering wheel. I feel sick. I discretely stuff what articles I can into my rucksack and race out of the library.

The fresh air hits me and I feel the vomit begin to whirl up inside. I duck around the corner into the alleyway between the council building and the library and hurl behind the bins. I'm surprised by how much comes out of me considering I haven't eaten. I wipe my sleeve across my mouth and push the hair from my face.

At the other end of the alleyway a figure, all in black, catches my eye. I quickly straighten out my clothes and pull my bag back onto my shoulder but when I look up again, they are gone. I leave the alley feeling weak and wobble back to the bus stop. I spend the entire journey willing myself not to throw up again, and every time I swallow there is a burning bitter taste like sour apples. When I get home, Julia is at the door looking worried. At first, I fear the worst, she is wearing the same face my parents had when they told me about Aunt Jenna.

'Miss Darcie, you better come inside. There are some policemen here to see you. They want to know where you were last night.'

My stomach tightens.

9: JJ

In the dream it's just me and my mum. We're holding hands and laughing, and I think we're laughing because our feet are not on the ground where they should be. We are floating and spinning, our hair swirling out around us, weaving in and out of smoky mist.

I wake when the duvet is ripped from my bed and a rough hand shakes my shoulder.

'Oi, wakey wakey, you little shit, I need to talk to you.'

I open my eyes and see Uncle Henry leaning over me, his eyes cold and his lips pulled into a sneer. This does not look good. I struggle into an upright position and rub at my face to wake myself up. Before I can even speak, he grabs the front of my t-shirt and pushes his face into mine.

'You said you sorted that Wheeler kid out last night, that right?'

I nod. 'Yeah, I did like you said.'

Henry tightens his hand, knotting the t-shirt around his fist. 'Did I say smash his head in, JJ? Did I say attack him in the public toilets and knock him unconscious? Did I say to do that?'

'No,' I sputter, shaking my head. I really don't like the look in his eyes. 'You said to get him alone, to take him down…'

He looks at me in utter disgust and runs his free hand through his thick hair. 'You've fucking done it now, do you know that? I just heard from Mac. He heard it in town this morning and called me. The Wheeler kid is in hospital, JJ, with a fractured bloody skull!'

I swallow thickly and start to panic when I see the mist again, rising from my hands. If Uncle Henry sees that… I try to ignore it and look into his eyes. 'I'm sorry, I didn't mean to put him in hospital, Uncle Henry. I swear!'

He bites his lip and shakes his head. He grips my t-shirt tighter. 'What the hell happened? What did you do to him, JJ?'

'I just punched him!' I throw up my hands and that's a mistake because the mist grows darker and swirls in the air around them. Oh, Jesus Christ, what the hell is this? What is wrong with me?

Uncle Henry is still shaking his head. He finally lets go of my t-shirt and steps back from my bed and for a moment he can't seem to bring himself to even look at me. He just stands there with one hand on his hip and the other touching his head, like he is trying to figure something out. Maybe this will be it, I think, maybe this will be the line I crossed, the one step too far he's always talking about. This will be when he calls children's services and finally gets shot of me.

'What did you hit him with?' he asks me.

'My hands, just my hands, I swear.'

'Jesus Christ, he must've hit his head on the floor or the sinks or something.' Uncle Henry presses both his hands against his face and drags them slowly down it. 'The police are going to turn up here, you know that don't you?'

I shrug, still sat in bed in my t-shirt and boxers, still trying like hell not to react to the black smoke circling my clenched fists.

'Nobody saw,' I tell him.

Uncle Henry scratches his head. 'What about that girl? What about her? Is that why you brought her back here, eh? Was she there too?'

I shake my head adamantly. 'No, I mean yes, she was there, but she didn't see anything, I promise. She ran off after I came in the toilet.'

He glares at me. 'She was in the toilet? With Jared?'

'Yes, he was attacking her, I don't know, assaulting her or something. I came in and he stopped, and she ran out and I…' I shrug my shoulders again, staring back at him in utter desperation. Because I want him to calm down, I want him to sit on the bed beside me and tell me it's going to be okay, because last night when I told him what I did, he was happy, he called me his boy!

'He was *attacking* her?'

'Yes, yes, you can ask her. I'll call her, I'll find her, I'll get her to tell you!'

Uncle Henry paces around the edge of my room. 'Jesus Christ, if that's true, you did the right thing, but you went too far, JJ, *that's* the problem!' And now he's stopped pacing and he's glaring at me again in a way I find all too familiar. Like he resents me, hates me, fears me and pities me all at once. The turmoil is all over his face and I can't hate him back when he looks at me like that because I know how much he loved his older brother. I know how devastated he still is, how angry he is with my mum. I know.

'I honestly just punched him,' I say. 'I just punched him, Uncle Henry. I'm sorry. I thought you wanted me to.'

He licks his lips and sighs heavily. 'Yeah. Well. Maybe there's no need for anymore sessions in the barn. You're obviously quite capable of taking care of one bully. What about the other kids? He had friends there, Mac said. They called the ambulance.'

I shake my head in response. 'No, they didn't see me, I'm sure of it. Just Darcie, and I'll talk to her, I swear.'

He nods. 'But the police will come here if Jared talks. It won't look good, JJ, not after what your mum did.'

He turns around when he says it because he can barely stand to say her name or mention her without wanting to be sick or wreck something.

Before he leaves, he looks back but not at me. 'You're not seeing her next month, okay? No arguments. No visit. It's no good for you seeing her.'

He walks out and slams the door behind him.

I sit there for a minute, not moving, barely breathing. I listen to him moving around the house, collecting his keys, answering his phone and telling Mac he's just coming. Then he leaves the house with Chester, slamming another door on me and I know if I get up and look out the window, he will be climbing into the Land Rover, still talking on his phone with that pinched, stressed look on his face.

He's gone. I look down at my hands, shaking uncontrollably and the mist is fainter, like grey smoke, softly circling and weaving its way between my fingers. It feels cold and empty and suddenly I just can't bear it. I get up and storm over to the dresser where my mum's stupid empty jar still sits collecting nothing. I seize it and hurl it at the wall. I want rid of it. I want rid of the crazy stuff she planted in my head. Sometimes, I want rid of *her...*

The jar smashes into several pieces on the floor and I throw myself back on the bed, my hands covering my face as I try and fail to stifle pointless tears. It's not Jared Wheeler I care about; I feel nothing for him. But if the police turn up? If he told them it was me? Uncle Henry was right - it won't look good after what my mother did. People already look at me like I might explode at any moment. I don't think I could bear it if it got any worse.

And as for this fucking mist! What the hell is it? Am I going mad? Am I already like her? Is it too late? Maybe I should just pack a bag and run. It would be better for everyone.

I'm seriously considering this when my phone starts to ring. I reach under my pillow and drag it out, noting instantly that the battery warning light is flashing at me. There is an unknown number calling and I'm scared. What if it's the police? Or Jared? Or his family?

I hold it in my hand, feeling the heat of it warm my palm, easing away the frigid cold of the dissipating mist. In a sudden fit of just fuck it all, I answer it.

'Hello?'

'JJ? Is that you?'

Jesus Christ, Darcie? I run a hand back through my hair and hold on. 'Yeah?'

'It's Darcie. I hope it's okay to call you.'

'Um… yeah. How did you even get my number?'

'Research,' she replies. 'I really need to see you. Like, *urgently*, as soon as you can.'

I want to ask why but I guess I already know. I sigh and start to look around my room for some clean clothes to pull on. 'Okay, where?'

There is a slight pause and I think I can hear rustling, like she is either packing a bag or putting on a jacket.

'How about the school field?' she suggests. 'That cluster of trees near the staff carpark? Can you get there now?'

'Yeah,' I tell her, fishing a clean t-shirt from the back of my chair. 'I'll be there.'

I hang up the phone, get dressed and I'm about to leave the house with some kind of purpose for once, when the house phone rings. Christ. I have to answer it in case it's

Uncle Henry wanting me to do something. I haven't done any of my chores yet but I'm hoping if I'm quick seeing Darcie, I can get back before him and do them.

I grab the phone from the hook in the hallway as I'm shoving my feet into trainers. 'Hello?'

'Hey!' sings a familiar voice, one that instantly drags my heart to the floor and stamps all over it. 'It's me, how are you, honey?'

Mum.

I can't do this now… I can't…

While I search and fight for something to say, for a way to tell her, to let her down gently, my fingers move over the handset and before I can say a word, I have hung up on her. Shit. I really hope she thinks we just got cut off.

10: Darcie

'Come on, JJ. Where the fuck are you?'

I am standing under the cover of trees across from the staff carpark, pacing back and forth and biting my bottom lip. A car rolls by and my heart skips a beat. Nope. Not him. I glance down at my phone and triple check the time. He should be here by now. Maybe something happened to him? Maybe the police got to him first? Maybe he doesn't take me seriously, just like everyone else?

Arms folded I march forward out from under the trees and take one last glance along the road. *That's it. Time's up.* I walk back and bend down to pick up my rucksack when a voice from behind me makes me jump right out of my skin.

'Holy *shit*, JJ!' I hiss as I drop my bag and run towards him, shoving him so hard in the chest that I fear he'll topple right over with me landing on top. I blush at the thought and for a moment find myself shocked at the firmness of his chest beneath his shirt. 'Where have you been? It's been ages!'

'Sorry. I was...' His eyes glaze over, and I can tell there is something he is wrestling with.

'It's fine. You're here now and that's all that matters.'

'So, what's so urgent?' He brushes his golden hair from his eyes, adjusts his glasses and leans back against a tree. One foot propped up on the bark with his hands in the pockets of his jeans.

'The police came to my house today!'

'Right...'

How is this not alarming to him? I suspect it is but he's trying to keep his cool.

'Right, so… They were asking me about last night… About the almost dead arsehole in the toilet block… JJ, why aren't you listening to me!?' He's removing a small sketch pad from his back pocket, and I snatch it from his hand.

'Hey!'

'JJ!'

'What? Look, it doesn't matter, okay. We just need to stay calm. We didn't do anything wrong. Besides, he deserved it.' He pulls away from the tree and kicks a rock across the ground. I want to tell him that he's wrong—that nobody deserves what Jared Wheeler went through. But I can't. As awful as it might make me sound, I agree with him. Jared deserves all that and more. He deserves it for everything he's put JJ through… every name he's called him, every punch he's thrown. He deserves it for what he did to me, or at least tried to, and to all the other countless girls that are probably too afraid to say anything… All those girls who didn't have JJ Carson there to save them.

'Look, forget me for a second. Forget Jared and how much of an asshat he is. I'm worried about you, JJ.' I walk over and place a hand on his arm. His eyes meet mine and there's something in them, burning beneath the darkness. I know he cares. Deep down I know he does.

'I'm fine,' he lies. 'You don't need to worry about me.'

He starts to walk away but stops dead when the next words leave my lips. 'They were asking me a lot of questions, you know. About Jared. About you. About your mother.'

Silence.

'I know what happened to her JJ… It was that mist wasn't it? And don't lie to me. I know you know I can see it too.'

56

He stands there like stone… The boy who saved my life, the boy from the river, the boy who watched his mother being wrenched away in handcuffs.

'I know you'll think I couldn't possibly understand it. I mean how could I right? I'm a Duffield. What could I possibly know about pain? But trust me, my life is nowhere near as perfect as it seems.' I hand the sketch pad back to him. 'I lost someone I care about too… The one person in the entire world that made me feel normal… Until you that is.'

He turns to face me, his bottom lip trembling.

'You can trust me, JJ.' I dare to step closer, reaching out a hand.

'I do.' His words are barely a whisper as his fingers reach out towards mine.

Then, the silence between us is shattered by the screeching of tyres. Someone's coming, and they're coming fast. JJ, instinctively I think, grabs my arm and pulls me behind a tree. We crouch into the dirt, my face buried into his back, but now I can see it once more, that strange black mist swirling out from his fingers as he digs them into the bark.

'Stay low,' he warns, 'it could be Jared's goons.'

'What if it's not?' I breathe against his neck. 'What if it's the police?'

'Even more reason to stay hidden.'

Before I know what has happened my arms are around his shoulders, hugging him tightly. My heartbeat thumping underneath my skin. I'm almost certain you can hear it echoing through the branches above. I look out into the vast field behind us… the trees, the birds… Could this be it? The last thing I see before I'm hauled off to prison for perverting the course of justice.

Perverting… How's that for irony?

Across the way I think I see someone watching us. At first, I wonder if it's Ben. I texted him last night explaining that things wouldn't work out between us anymore, and I've been dodging his calls ever since. The figure moves closer and I notice it's the same person from the alleyway beside the library. Now, from the roadside, I hear the slam of a car door. The heavy crunch of footsteps drawing near. I squeeze my eyes shut and nestle into JJ.

'Oi, you two. In the car, now!'

*

'I've been looking all over for you.' JJ's uncle Henry places a mug of tea down on the table in front of me, before moving around to the other side and leaning against it with both hands. I sit still like a naughty school kid, my hands in my lap. I go to thank him for the tea, but he cuts me off, his eyes firmly planted on his nephew.

'Guess who ran into Mr Wheeler this morning. It's worse than I thought, JJ. They're starting a full-on appeal to find witnesses. They're on about pressing some serious charges. Said they'd send the person responsible straight to the gallows if they could.'

Henry glances at me, then to the ceramic biscuit barrel in the centre of the table. He slides it towards me with a meaty hand.

'No, no. Thank you. I'm fine.'

'What is it with you young girls?' he huffs. 'Go on, take one. You worried it'll go straight to your hips or something?' He laughs and I keep my eyes down on my hands. JJ clears his throat and pulls away the barrel. I peer up in time to see the warning glare he dares to throw his uncle's way. *Wow, am I really that obvious?* Henry stands up straight and for a moment I think he is going to apologise but he doesn't.

'Listen, erm, Miss Duffield–'

'Darcie,' JJ cuts in.

'Darcie, my nephew here tells me that he only did what he did to the Wheeler kid because, well…' He swallows hard. 'Because…'

I know what he wants to say. He wants to say Jared was trying to assault me. He wants me to relive it now and confirm that it's true. But I'm not sure that I can. I have already spent the entire night in and out of that toilet block in my dreams. I can't go back there. I just can't. But then I look across and see JJ. He's staring down at the table in silence, his lip quivering slightly. I think about all the shit that Jared put us both through. I think about how difficult it must be living here with his father's brother. I feel bad for him. I want to protect him, keep him safe, and to do that I have to tell the truth.

I fight back tears as I look up into Henry's eyes and tell him exactly what happened that night. I tell him everything from Vicky's party right up until the point of JJ rescuing me. I tell him every single thing there is to know, apart from the one thing I know I must keep hidden—the presence of the thick black mist.

Henry takes a seat opposite us and lets out a sigh, placing his hands against his temples. For a moment there is the longest silence, until finally he speaks.

'So, here's what we're gonna do…'

11: JJ

Uncle Henry tells us his plan. He sits and tells us exactly what we should do and how we should act. It's terrifying and amazing. Surely, he should see this as his chance to finally get rid of me? Tell the police it was me, tell children's services he can't cope? But he doesn't take the chance to get shot of me. He helps me.

'I'll give JJ an alibi,' he states calmly, looking from me to Darcie and back again. 'The boys were drunk as hell last night, so they won't remember whether you were here the whole time or came back with Darcie. Besides, they'd back me up in a heartbeat, any time. Mac and Rich were best friends with your dad, JJ. They wouldn't see you in the shit, okay?'

I glance at Darcie before nodding nervously. 'Okay.'

Uncle Henry sighs again and focuses on Darcie. 'Obviously, your mates know you were there, and they'll know you wandered off at some point. What did you tell the police already, Darcie?'

She takes a deep breath before starting. 'I told them I left early, alone. That's it.'

'You didn't tell them you were in the toilet block with Jared?'

She shakes her head grimly. 'No. No one knows.'

'Okay,' Uncle Henry smiles very faintly before running a hand back through his hair and sitting back. 'It's a damn shame no one will ever know what he tried to do to you but he's not gonna say you or JJ were there, or he dumps himself in it, right?'

Darcie and I look at each other and then shrug back at Henry. 'Right,' I reply.

Henry claps his hands together. 'There we go then. We should be fine.'

'Okay,' Darcie nods, looking relieved but a little unsure.

Uncle Henry rolls his eyes as if it's all been a terrific headache and inconvenience to him and gets up from the table. He points a finger at me. 'You. Didn't do your chores. Hop to it. Now.' He gives Darcie a nod and a wink. 'See you later, sweetheart.'

I can't help flinching. *Sweetheart?*

Uncle Henry walks out and leaves us alone. I wince at Darcie. 'Sorry but I gotta do a load of stuff around here.'

'I really need to talk to you,' she says, following as I leave the table and slip out the front door.

I shrug. 'Okay, so talk.'

I stomp across the farmyard until I reach the cow barn. Darcie follows, hurrying to keep pace with me. I yank open the barn door and the smell of cow dung hits us in the eyes. Darcie recoils slightly and then laughs.

'Lovely!'

'Look, you can go,' I tell her. 'You heard Uncle Henry. It should be fine as long as we keep to the story and Jared doesn't talk. And he won't talk, will he?'

She shakes her head solemnly, her long blonde ponytail flicking from one shoulder to the other. 'I don't think so but that's not what I want to talk about, JJ.'

'What then?' I frown and duck through the door.

The cows are all out to pasture but their barn reeks and is full of random chickens. I grab a big rake that's leaning against the wall and start to drag the piles of shitty straw into a pile. How can she want to hang around for this? But she does. It seems like when this girl gets a bee in her bonnet, she doesn't like to let go. I smile a little then, as she reminds me of a nosy reporter, you know, someone like Lois Lane. And then there's me, with the black mist… like a superhero. She must see my smile because she comes closer.

'What's so funny?'

'Nothing.'

'Come on,' she urges, with her own playful smile, 'what's with this constant silent act anyway? It's almost like you don't want to make friends.'

'Oh, I tried,' I tell her, looking up. 'When I moved here, I tried like hell to put the past behind me and just get on with stuff like my uncle wanted me to. But people around here couldn't let me.' I look back at the muck and shrug my shoulders. 'You saw what Jared and those other kids were like. It's been like that for me since I got here so excuse me if I've given up trying to fit in.'

Darcie folds her arms and looks me up and down. 'All right, fair enough. But you don't need to fit in with me anyway. We've got stuff to talk about, right?'

I turn in a slow circle, dragging the shit with me, biting at my lower lip. I'm not sure I want her to say it again. If Darcie saw the mist too, that makes it real and I am not sure what is worse - me being crazy or the mist being real.

'The smoke, JJ,' she sighs from behind me. 'The mist, whatever it is. The first time I thought I imagined it. I thought I was seeing things, or it was a cigarette butt or something. And then with Jared?' She steps closer, her voice dropping. 'I couldn't even see your hands. They were totally smothered and it… did something to you, right?'

I'm scared…so scared. I want to turn and run. I want to scream at her to get out and never come near me again. Now that Jared isn't a problem anymore, maybe it will never happen again and I can just get back to being weird JJ Carson nobody talks to. But if I admit it? If I turn around and look her in the eye and *trust* her?

Shit, it feels like the hardest thing in the world.

'JJ,' she snaps at me then and I swear I hear her stamp her foot. Another smile wants to break free, but I don't let it. 'You can ignore me all you want. You can push me away and shut me out, but it won't work, okay? I should warn you that I'm very stubborn, just like my Aunt Jenna was actually. Very, very stubborn. And I'll just keep showing up here and I'm sure your uncle will be happy to let me in. And I'll just keep asking you and asking you until you break.'

'Jesus,' I turn to face her and fold my arms on top of the rake. 'Ask me what, Darcie? What?'

'The black mist,' she insists, and her cheeks are all flushed, and her jaw is tight. She's getting mad and I kind of like it. 'We were talking about it before Henry showed up and we're gonna talk about it now.'

I nod at her reluctantly. 'Did anyone ever tell you you're really annoying?'

'Not recently,' she replies with a toss of her ponytail, 'but after all the Jared stuff I think I'm now a social outcast like you. So, we might as well stick together, what do you say?'

Jesus Christ…This girl.

I lift a hand and drop it in defeat. 'Okay then.'

'When did it first happen?' she asks, not missing a beat. 'The mist around your hands.'

'I've seen it before,' I tell her, 'but not in the same way. I mean, I thought I was imagining it before because it was just on the paper before I drew.'

She steps closer. 'What do you mean?'

'I don't know, it was just there but really faint, like a shadow, like it was trying to show me what to draw.'

'And it didn't come from your hands?'

I shake my head. 'No. No way. It was just there sometimes and I just, I don't know, I didn't think it was real. And then the other day, it showed up when I realised my mum's jar was empty. I mean, it was *in* the jar!'

'What jar?'

'It's a long story,' I groan. 'But my mum, who you obviously know is crazy, before she got locked up, she gave me this old jar that her mum gave her, and it's like some weird family heirloom or folk story or whatever. Anyway, the idea is you keep it full of things that make you smile. Like, I dunno, love letters or flowers or trinkets or some other dumb shit.'

'Nice,' she nods at me. 'I like that. It makes sense. Gives you things to be positive about.'

I roll my eyes and return to the raking of cow shit. 'Whatever. Anyway, I did it to please her. I put pennies in it and sweets and stuff and recently some dandelions because they reminded me of her. Then they vanished. I think Uncle Henry swiped them. And that's when the mist started to show up.'

'Wow,' Darcie breathes, shaking her head at me. 'That's a weird coincidence. What else did she say about this jar? Could it be cursed or magic or something?'

I stop raking and glare at her. 'You don't really believe in stuff like that, do you?'

'I dunno. I'm just trying to get to the bottom of this. What else did she say?'

'She said you had to keep it full all the time or the empty would get you,' I roll my eyes again so that Darcie knows how crazy I think this is.

'The empty?'

'Something like that.'

'And once the jar was empty, the mist came?'

I groan at her. 'Yeah, but it can't be. I mean…' I throw the rake down and place my hands on my hips. 'That's just crazy.'

She nods, but her eyes are full of wondering. She gazes around the barn as if trying to think up some logical explanation. 'What does it feel like?' she asks me then. 'When the mist comes? Can you control it?'

'It feels cold,' I tell her, thinking back to that moment in the toilet block with Jared. 'Then it feels… powerful, I guess.'

'Could you have done that to Jared normally?'

I nod at the punch bag hanging on the other side of the barn. 'My uncle makes me attack that thing nearly every day. He was embarrassed of me getting my arse kicked so he kept making me box. I know how to defend myself, Darcie, it's just it was always three of them. I couldn't beat three of them.'

Darcie is nodding her head and biting her lip. She doesn't look at me and my paranoia seeps in and tells me it's because she's starting to realise what a fucked-up loser I am. She gazes at the door and I can tell she wants to leave.

'You'll be doing this a while?' she asks, nodding at the cow dung.

'Oh yeah.'

'I'll be back later then,' and with that she stalks back towards the door, moving fast, her stride purposeful and her ponytail swinging.

'Where're you going?' I call after her.

'My favourite place!' she smiles back over her shoulder. 'Keep your phone charged up. I'll call you later, okay?'

When she's gone, I stare at the muck for a while, trying to figure out what the hell just happened. I realise one thing right away - I really like talking to Darcie Duffield.

12: Darcie

I take a deep breath as I step into the foyer of the library and I can't help but smile. This is all very exciting. Finally, for a brief moment in time I feel as if I am part of something bigger. Some higher purpose. JJ needs me to get to the bottom of what is happening to him and heaven knows I clearly need him too. I mean, who else is there?

The library is busier than usual. I watch as people scurry between the stacks like ants, hungry for their next hit of adventure, desperate for another crumb of knowledge they can smuggle back to the hive. Flicking from face to face I can't help but notice that I am by far the youngest one here. Most kids my age would rather search for something on their phone than even dream of stepping foot in here, but even if I wanted to, what would I search? '*Strange black mist produced by humans*'? I shake my head as I stroll over to the front desk where I'm greeted by a flustered looking librarian.

'Hello, dear. Can I help you?' She is wrestling with a pile of volumes that threaten to topple onto the floor at any moment. I reach out a hand to steady them just in time. 'Ooh, thank you. That was close.'

I smile. 'Um, I was wondering if you had any books on superpowers?'

She looks at me confused for a second then smiles back. 'Comic books are over there, dear.'

'Oh, no… Sorry, I mean…' *What do I mean exactly?*

I wrack my brain for an answer before I continue. 'Do you have anything on local folklore? Myths and legends… That sort of thing.'

'Certainly.' She guides me over to a small section in the centre of the library. 'Anything particular you are after?'

'Black mist,' I say without thinking.

'Black mist… Hmmm, can't say I know anything about that.' She looks me up and down like I might shatter apart at any moment.

'That's okay, I'm sure I'll find something.'

She flashes me one last smile and begins to waddle back to her place behind the desk. 'Americans…' I hear her mutter beneath her breath with a chuckle.

I run a finger along the colourful spines in front of me. There isn't much here at all but enough for me to spend a good few hours researching. I gather what I can into my arms and carry them over to the nearest table, sprawling them out in front of me.

'Right,' I sigh, tugging my ponytail tighter and smoothing out my jeans before taking a seat. 'Let's do this.'

*

Three and a half hours.

Three and a half hours and around twenty-eight books.

Nothing.

Not one single thing about strange black mists. To say I am disappointed would be a serious understatement. I slam the last book shut and toss it on the pile, leaning back in my chair and chewing my bottom lip. *Now what?* I attempt to carry the books back to their designated area, but an employee stops me and insists on doing it on my behalf. There it is again, the perks of being a Duffield. *Can't I ever do anything for myself?*

Outside, I am pleased to find that the sun is still burning bright and strong and I begin a steady stroll towards the bus stop. I'm disappointed, but if there's one thing Aunt Jenna taught me, it's to never give up. I will find the answers. I know it. I have to know it or what will that mean for JJ? What will that mean for me?

I'm almost at the stop when I see it. That sleek black dress and bouffant hair accompanied by the familiar *click clack* of Jimmy Choos against the pavement. *Mother.*

'Darcie? Sweetheart, what on earth…' She glances up at the bus stop and back to me. 'Sweetheart, you're not thinking of taking *the bus*, are you?' I smirk at the way she mumbles when she says *'the bus'* as if it's a dirty word.

'Hi Mom,' I grumble.

'Honey, absolutely not. Come with me, I have the car parked behind M and S. You can't possibly be seen on the bus. Especially not wearing that.' She angles her sunglasses down so she can better scrutinise my outfit. 'I'll ask Julia to pick you up some new clothes, you can't go around wearing something so tight, Darcie. You're practically bursting at the seams.'

I feel embarrassed. Heavy. I thought I looked perfectly fine in the mirror this morning. The girl inside the glass seemed to approve, and JJ didn't seem to mind the way I looked. Come to think of it, neither did his uncle Henry. Then, just when I feel like things can't get any worse, I hear my mother speak five gut-wrenching words.

'Victoria Marshall, is that you?'

I cringe. I haven't seen Vicky since that night at the park and I have no idea if she feels I'm responsible. *Has Jared spoken to her? Did she see me enter the toilet block?*

'Hi, Mrs D.' I turn to face her, she's wearing a hot pink crop top, baggy yoga pants and snapping on her bubble gum. 'Oh, hi DeeDee. Didn't see you there.'

'How could you miss her?' My mother grumbles under her breath, smoothing out her dress. I scowl at her, but she isn't paying attention to me, she's already lost in some shop window. There's an awkward pause until she finally speaks again, still without looking back at us. I notice the girl reflected in the glass next to her. My mother's right. What was I thinking wearing this? I'm hideous. My stomach twists and the girl in the reflection seems to smile.

'Victoria, dear. Why don't you come over to the house tonight for dinner? We haven't seen you for ages.'

'Mom, I don't think Vicky would-'

'Don't be rude, Darcie.'

My lips are immediately glued shut. I dare to lift my eyes towards Vicky, and I'm surprised to see that instead of a smug grin she looks just as awkward as I must, shifting uncomfortably in her ballet flats.

'That would be nice.' I'm floored. 'DeeDee and I need to catch up anyway.'

'We do?' There's a look between us and I am not sure what to make of it. *Is she testing me? Does she know that I had something to do with what happened to Jared Wheeler? What if she's seen me about with JJ and wants to interrogate me?*

My mother offers to drop Vicky back home and I am relieved to hear that she is heading into town to meet the other girls; though I am certain I will be the topic of conversation. The drive home is only short, and I can't wait to leave the car - I have never felt so uncomfortable. Back home, I shrug off my jacket and hang it over the banister. I climb the stairs, defeated, when I hear Jeremy screaming at the TV in his room. I hover in the doorway watching and he spots me in his peripheral.

'Hi, squirt,' I smile. I feel bad for Jeremy, I should really give him more attention. Make sure he's okay so that he doesn't end up like me.

'Oh, hey.'

'Whatcha doing kid?'

'Nothing. Just playing.' He nods towards the TV. 'Wanna join?'

I walk in and crash down on the beanbag chair next to his bed. He logs me in and hands me the spare controller.

'You can be Jade. She's pretty badass.'

'Perfect.'

The game loads and we begin mashing the keys. At first, I'm in the lead, then I notice something strange about his character—there's an ominous black mist permeating from his fists. When I go to strike him with a flying kick to the face he disappears into a puff of smoke, reappearing behind me. He smacks me hard in the back and delivers his finishing move. A deep voiced narrator booms through the speakers, '*Smoke wins!*' I drop my controller.

'Hey, Jer… Who's that?'

'Him? Oh, that's Smoke. He's awesome.'

'Smoke…?'

'Yeah, I did this report on him for my English homework. He's so cool. He's an Enenra.'

'A what?'

'An Enenra. It's Japanese. There's a book over there about them.' He nods towards his chest of drawers, but his eyes are back on the screen and he is already engrossed in the next match. I walk over and begin flipping through the pages. I feel like the world has blown out around me as I digest the words.

Enenras are dark beings who take the form of a mist-like substance, though they can often take human form. Some are born human whilst others are reincarnations of deceased human souls. They are only visible to those of the purest heart.

I run my finger along the illustrations on the neighbouring page - it shows a human figure in four different stages. The fourth is almost entirely consumed in darkness and there is a bold Japanese symbol stamped across it. I've seen this symbol before; it was in one of the books back at the library, I'm sure of it.

'Do you mind if I borrow this?'

My brother grunts and continues to mash the keys. I take that as an 'okay'.

Back in my room I perch on the end of the bed, open my laptop, and begin scouring the internet for the strange symbol. It takes a while but eventually I find it and my heart hits the floor. *Shinigami: Death Bringer.*

My hand instinctively flutters to my phone and I scroll through, stopping on JJ Carson. Then, right before I click dial, I stop. My heart is crying out to me, pleading with me to call him, to warn him about what might happen if he doesn't control the mist now, stop it in its tracks. But I can't. I can't call JJ now and start worrying him when I am not even sure about what I'm reading myself. I glance up at the girl in the mirror and for once she agrees. I drop my phone back onto the bedspread and rub my hands against my face. No matter what, I am sure of one thing— something very dark is taking hold of JJ Carson, changing him from the inside out, and I have to stop it before it does.

13: JJ

After cleaning out the barn, I head back into the house and my mind is spinning. It's all full of Darcie and the mist and my mum and there's a part of me that feels warm for once, knowing that someone cares. I remember to charge up my phone in case she calls me back and then I start sweeping up the broken jar.

Instantly, regret swamps me. I shouldn't have smashed it like that. Whether it meant anything to me or not was not the point; it obviously meant something to my mother and her mother before that. It's not like I have anything else to remember her by, anything else to hold on to. I feel bad about hanging up on her too and I know I'll have to deal with that situation at some point. But there's Uncle Henry to consider in all this. He was good to take me in, no one can argue with that and of course I can understand why he wouldn't want me seeing her. She killed his brother… Anyone would feel the same.

I'm mulling this all over and hoping my phone goes off, when the door opens and Uncle Henry appears. He squints at the glass in the dustpan. 'What was that?'

I wave a hand and get to my feet. 'Just that jar my mum left me. I knocked it over by accident.'

Uncle Henry looks like he wants to say something about the jar, but he doesn't. His jaw snaps shut, and he exhales thoughtfully, before beckoning me with one finger. 'C'mere a minute.'

I follow him out of my room and as he walks down the stairs, he throws a look over his shoulder. 'You're not busy or anything?'

'No, just waiting for a call,' I shrug.

I'm wondering what he's going to say when he opens the hall cupboard and drags out the vacuum cleaner that sits in there collecting dust.

'Clean this place up for me, would you?' he says, abruptly, sliding it across the hall floor towards me. 'I've got that waitress coming on over tonight.'

I'm confused. 'Waitress?'

'Yeah,' he says, slipping into the kitchen. I follow and watch in dumb silence as he shoves a load of our dirty washing into the machine and slams the door. 'And this too,' he adds, not looking at me. 'You know how to do it. About time you pulled your weight a bit more.'

I swallow the lump in my throat and nod at him. 'Sure, no problem, Uncle Henry. You really like her then, hey?'

To this, he lifts his upper lip and shakes his head in something similar to disgust. He barges back past me and into the hall where he fetches his keys from the hook. Chester is already panting at the front door, knowing he will be going along for the ride.

'Don't even know her name,' says Uncle Henry.

'Oh.'

He waves his hand around the house and does not look at me as he says, 'all of it, okay? It's got in a right state lately and you know I'm too busy with the farm to keep up with it. When I get back with her at eight, I expect it spotless, right? And you'll be out.'

Out? I think of Darcie and hope and pray that she calls me back before then. Otherwise it's back to wandering the streets like a loser.

'Of course,' I tell him, forcing a smile. 'And hey, Uncle Henry, I didn't get a chance to thank you properly. You know for saving our arses today and everything.'

He's at the door, Chester at his side and he pauses and looks back at me. His expression now is so different to the one he had earlier, when he was offering Darcie biscuits and joking about girls always being on diets. He looks at me like I am a stranger, like I am no one, nothing. He looks right through me and it makes me feel like I am invisible to him.

'I shouldn't have had to,' he growls, head lowered. 'You went too far, JJ. Don't do it again.'

I shouldn't argue with him but in that moment, I just can't help it. After all those sessions in the barn, him making me punch that bag, making me spar with him, yelling at me when I got it wrong, calling me a pussy and a girl, telling me it was all for my own good to make me strong so these people wouldn't walk all over me… I just did what he wanted, didn't I?

'I fought back, Uncle Henry,' I say, softly. 'They were kicking my arse every day, you know that. I just did like you said, and I put a stop to it.'

He sniffs and shakes his head hard. 'No. Not like that. You went too far and you know it. Something's not right about that whole story. *You* putting a bigger kid in hospital does not look good to me, not after what your mother did.'

Oh Christ, so we're back to that? Every time it comes back to that. Why the hell did he take me in if that was how he felt? He should never have bothered.

'It's not the same,' I argue, teeth clenched.

'Yes, it is,' Uncle Henry steps forward. 'She was fine until that day, wasn't she? You remember, right? Head in the clouds scatterbrain but not a bad bone in her, right?' He steps closer again and leans towards me. 'Right?' he yells.

'Right, but…'

75

'Then she *snaps*,' he says, clicking his fingers in my face and making me jump, 'just like that. No warning.' Uncle Henry holds up his hands in mock surrender. 'I'm just saying, JJ, it makes me a little bit nervous, that's all.'

I shake my head at him. I feel a tingling in my hands and when I dare to look down, I can see the mist is back, just grey for now and spiralling between my fingers like puffs of smoke.

'But Dad was cheating on her. You told me that yourself. She found out and she was so upset… she…'

Now Uncle Henry laughs at me. He throws back his head and laughs as he turns and struts back to the door, and I think, this is the real Henry Carson, this is the Henry he hides from everyone else; this is the Henry he even hid from Darcie. No one knows this cruel, dark side to him, but me. And what have I done to deserve it? I haven't killed anyone!

'And that makes it okay, does it?' he bellows from the door as he opens it and lets Chester run out. 'So, if Darcie spends some time with another boy, you're gonna attack her with a hammer, are you? You're gonna flip out like your mum did?'

My jaw drops open. I cannot believe he just said that to me. My hands are getting colder and the skin is going numb. I don't look at them, but I know if I did the mist would be darker now, nearly black.

Uncle Henry, the real Henry, looks me up and down like I am nothing but a piece of shit on his shoe. 'Just shut your stupid mouth, JJ and get on with cleaning this place up.' He turns and slams the door so hard the glass in the window shakes.

I stand there for a while, breathing hard with something thrumming and beating inside my chest like it's desperate to get out. And then I turn and lay my hands on the nearest thing to me which happens to be the TV set. Suddenly I am wrenching it away from the stand and hurling it right across the room. It feels like nothing, like a pillow or a feather - it's like I could have sent it across the room with just my fingertip.

The TV hits the hallway wall and smashes and the sound of tinkling glass seems to get through to me.

Shit, shit shit... He'll kill me, he'll kill me!

The mist evaporates as I rush into the hallway and set the TV upright. The screen is smashed to pieces - how the hell am I going to explain this? I pick it up and carry it back to the stand in the lounge. I position it front down on the floor, so it looks like I just knocked into it with something and sent it sprawling. It's plausible, just about. And then I go into a mad cleaning frenzy, because I have no choice, because he already hates me, *despises* me, probably wishes I was dead! Because if I get kicked out, where would I go? I'd have nothing, no one. And because he's right anyway, isn't he? Uncle Henry is right about everything, right about my mum and right about me! I *did* do that to Jared Wheeler, I beat him unconscious and Henry knows it, oh he knows it and that little display just now was his way of reminding me.

I hoover the entire house. I dust, I polish, I knock down cobwebs, I take out rubbish, I do two loads of washing and hang it all out to dry. I do the washing up and put all the clean dishes and cups away in the cupboards. And finally, I traipse upstairs, close to tears, sniffing like a baby, like a loser and I check my phone, and there is nothing.

It's seven now and I'll have to get out of here soon, for God knows how long. My finger trembles over her name but I can't do it, I can't press call. Instead, I drop on to the bed and pick up my notebook and pencil. Drawing always calms me down and Christ, I need to chill out before I see Uncle Henry again. I draw whatever comes into my head and I see it first on the paper before the pencil starts to move, almost without conscious thought. Uncle Henry's cold face, Darcie's swinging ponytail, the smashed TV set, and the smashed jar and around all of that, swirling and weaving and tightening its grip, the black mist.

At half past seven I check my phone one more time but there is nothing from Darcie. I feel a painful tightening in my guts and it's kind of hard to breathe.

She's forgotten about you, the intrusive thoughts tell me, as I pack a few things and leave the house to Henry and his waitress. *She's probably with Ben, she's having fun... Why would she call you anyway? Why would she give a shit about you?*

14: Darcie

Need to meet… NOW!

Delete.

JJ, I have news. Can you meet?

Delete.

JJ…

'Darcie, Dear. The sprouts?'

I slip my phone into my pocket and hand over the bowl. My mother has gone all out on this dinner. I've never seen so many green things in my life. There's asparagus, kale, and something else that I'm pretty sure shouldn't be this consistency. I stab at it with my fork, wondering for a moment if it will get up and walk away. Heaven knows I wish I could. Across from me Vicky is shovelling forkfuls of peas into her mouth, whilst Jeremy is arranging his into a smiley face. I turn my attention back to the alien substance on my plate.

'So, Victoria. What are your parents doing this summer? Any holiday plans?'

'Mum says she wants to go back to Thailand, but Dad's not too keen.'

'Bad time of year?'

'Too many spiders.'

I see my dad raise his eyebrows slightly and suppress a smirk. I smile. As much as I wish he wasn't so obsessed with work, I can't deny that his job is pretty cool. I mean, how many kids can say their dad is a head researcher at a big biological company? Spiders were the least of dad's worries. He must have seen it all in the lab. I bet he could tell me exactly what species this is. I stab at my plate again. *Or was.* I remember one time not long after we'd moved here, he came home ecstatic. Some huge top-secret breakthrough. I recall wondering why he even told us about it at all, only to then tell us he was not at liberty to discuss it any further. Of course, Jeremy and I had attempted to break into the home office to search through his files. But that was useless.

'Here I was thinking Mayor Marshall was a fearless warrior,' grins Dad.

'Oh, he is mostly. Just not with anything that has more legs than necessary,' Vicky beams mid-chew.

I stab at a roast potato and raise it to my lips. 'Dad, why don't you tell Vicky about the time you-' My mother clears her throat and I see her eyeing the potato, I allow it to drop back onto the plate and start over. 'You know, the time when-'

He's not listening to me. Nobody is listening to me. They are all far too preoccupied with their food; the clinking of cutlery and the occasional *'mmm'* the only sound. Then my dad looks up and starts asking Vicky about her college plans. I watch how invested he is when she says that she is interested in becoming a beautician, but she thinks she might stay on for sixth form like me.

'Good for you. If that's what you want to do, go for it I say.'

No way. No fucking way would he ever say that to me. Everything is always dictated. How I should dress, who I should be friends with, where I should go to university. I am sick of it. I feel the hurt bubble up inside of me and before I know it, I have shovelled three helpings of sweet potatoes into my mouth. I reach my fork for the roasties once more and ignore my mother's grunt of disapproval. I eat and I eat until I am fit to burst.

I excuse myself from the table after desert, Crème Brûlée, and storm up the stairs whilst Vicky helps my mother and Julia clear the table. I slump down on the floor by my bed and let out a silent scream, fists clenched into my hair. The girl in the mirror is smirking at me. She's laughing at me like I am weak. Pathetic. *No Darcie. Don't do it. Don't. You don't have to do it.* But the stress, guilt and disgust is rumbling away inside of me. It's scratching at my insides, forcing me into the en suite. I won't do it though. I won't. I'm better than that. I'm so much better. In my mind I see my mother's disapproving glance, my dad smiling at Vicky but seeing right through me like glass. I scramble to the toilet and before I know it the pain is gone, and I am free.

I return to my room a few minutes later, mopping at my chin with a hand towel when I notice someone hovering in the doorway. Their frame silhouetted by the glare of the hallway light behind them. *Holy shit, Vicky? How much did she hear?* I throw down the towel and move towards the door but as I do the figure comes into focus.

'Jeremy?' I place a hand on the doorframe and glance back over my shoulder at the en suite. 'What's up?'

'I came to get my book back. The one you took earlier. Chris wants to read it.'

'Right…' I grab the book from my bedside table and hand it back to him. I wait for him to leave but he lingers.

'You don't have to, you know.' His words are soft, and I notice he is looking past me, and not in that dismissive way like everyone else, but over my shoulder towards my bathroom. I see something deep and torturing in his eyes then, like he wants to help me, but he doesn't know how.

Vicky emerges at the top of the stairs and he slips past her in the narrow hall. 'I'm watching those hands, Jer,' she mocks as he brushes by. But he's not listening, his eyes are firmly fixed on me until he disappears down the stairs, out of view.

'So, DeeDee.' Vicky is in my room now, running her hand along the photographs pinned to my cork-board. She tugs one of Ben and I free and drops it into the wastepaper bin. 'Where've ya been?'

'What d'you mean?'

'Nobody's seen you since the park. You haven't even checked in on Jared.'

She sits on the end on my bed, and I think she is reaching into her pocket for a tissue, but she pulls out her lip gloss. Using the mirror as a guide she applies it and smacks her lips together. 'Can you believe someone just left him for dead on that filthy toilet floor? Ugh. So sad. Still, Mr Wheeler's promised to fly us all out to Tenerife after the trial to celebrate.'

'Trial?'

'Yeah. They're suing the council. Apparently, those toilets should have been torn down ages ago. A total death trap.'

'But I thought he was attacked?'

'Yeah, but still, if the floors weren't so bloody disgusting, he'd probably have been able to fight back. Of course, with Dad being the mayor it ruffled some feathers. But it's all cool now. He told Mr Wheeler if I was the one hurt, he'd do the exact same thing.' She turns her face from left to right, fluffing out her hair and drinking in her reflection.

'So, do the police have any leads?'

'Don't think so.'

'And Jared, does he remember anything?'

'Don't you think he'd tell the police if he did?'

I smile. I don't mean to and I pray to every God in existence that Vicky hasn't noticed. I can't believe we've done it; we've actually gotten away with it. The police aren't going to find any evidence now, not this late in the game. I am painfully aware of the phone in my pocket and I desperately want to wrench it out and call JJ.

'Listen, DeeDee, about the other night.' *Uh, oh. Here it comes.* 'I didn't mean to snap your head off like that. I was just super hormonal. I can't blame you for going after Jared. I mean, it's not like you're blind.' I roll my eyes, but she doesn't notice, she's too busy rifling through the stack of old magazines by my bed. 'Just remember to keep your hands to yourself in future, 'kay?'

'Deal.' I didn't want to say it, but I have to let her believe in whatever deluded fantasy she has going on in her mind. It's the only sure-fire way to keep this conversation short and sweet so I can get her out of my room. 'Listen, I have some stuff I have to do tonight, so…' I smile awkwardly and my eyes dart across to the door.

'Oh. That's fine. I've gotta get home soon anyway.'

I'm surprised by how easy it is to shift her. It's certainly not at all like the Vicky Marshall I know. But there's no point questioning it. I need to call JJ and tell him what I've learnt. Obviously, it's only a silly old myth but it's all we have to go on for now. I wait for Vicky to slink out of sight and dive for my phone.

Something's wrong. The call goes straight to voicemail. I leave him a brief message and decide to try the landline. I guess the signal must be terrible way out in the

83

countryside. This time I am relieved when I hear the beeping of the dial tone. A gruff voice answers.

'Yellow.'

'JJ?'

'Who's asking?'

'It's me, Darcie.'

'Oh, Miss Duffield.' I realise then that I am talking to JJ's uncle Henry. His voice immediately perks, and I swear I can hear someone giggling in the background. 'Sorry, JJ's not in.'

'Oh... Do you know where he is? I need to speak to him.'

'Your guess is as good as mine, kid. I can tell you one thing though, if you manage to find the little bastard send him right back here, will you? Little punk smashed up my TV.'

'Smashed your TV?'

'Another one of his little tantrums, I guess.'

'Okay, um, I'll be sure to tell him.'

'Good girl.' I hear the giggling once more and Henry says something that I can't quite catch before the line goes dead.

Shit.

Shit, shit, shit.

Not only is JJ not home but now I know he's upset, and if there is one thing we know for certain about that damn black mist, it's that it always seems to appear when he is angry, upset or hurting. I have to find him now before things get any worse. Smashing a TV is one thing but who knows what he'll do if he runs into Andrew Hart or Frankie Simpson. Without a second thought I fly down the stairs and out into the crisp evening air.

I run into town, checking every side alley and carpark on the way. I'm running so hard my feet ache and my chest is heaving. It feels as though my lungs will give up at any moment. I check the river path, the train station, even the school field. Nothing. JJ is nowhere to be seen. I try his phone once again but it's no use. I can't give up though. I won't. Then it hits me, as crazy as it sounds there is one place I have left to check. The park. Of course, returning to the scene of the crime might not be the smartest move, but it's certainly worth a shot.

My legs can barely carry me as I break through the gates, but I keep going. I glance towards the old toilet block in the corner and grimace. It's all covered with police tape and a big sign warns people to keep back. Whilst it is very possible that JJ could be inside, I can't go in. I just can't. Instead, I skirt passed the block and over to the old club house by the bowls green, confident I will find him there.

I call out his name through the broken window. No answer. The panic is increasing now. *What if something has happened to him? What if he's hurt? What if the mist has gotten hold of him and he's disappeared entirely?*

That's when I see it, a few soft wisps of black smoke rising up from the bandstand. I hurry towards it and sure enough there he is. Huddled down in the corner, sketch pad in hand, hurriedly scribbling away. He hasn't noticed me; he is far too immersed in his drawing and the mist is swirling around his hand as it darts across the page. I'm so relieved to see him that I don't even call his name, I simply run forwards and fling my arms around him. He drops the pencil as if I have broken him free from some magic spell, and slowly he sinks into my embrace.

'Darcie?'

'I'm so glad I found you. I'm so glad you're safe.'
Then I remember how I couldn't reach his phone, and just
how worried he'd made me. 'You. Asshole,' I say shoving
him away and then tugging him into a hug once more. I
pull back and laugh as I clock his expression, he looks
completely and utterly confused. I start to tell him about
how I'd been looking for him, and how his uncle Henry
had mentioned the smashed TV but a noise from the path
interrupts us.

'Well, well, well. So, this is what was so important.'

It's Vicky Marshall. Has she followed me here? She
steps out of the shadows so I can better see the smirk that
is painted across her face. 'Sorry, babes. I didn't want you to
find out like this,' she adds, glancing over her shoulder into
the gloom. *Who is she talking to?* I climb to my feet and then
my heart stops as I watch an angry looking Ben Evans step
out to join her.

15: JJ

For a horrible moment, all four of us just stare at each other and say nothing. The only one who looks pleased with herself is that God-awful Vicky Marshall. If anyone is perfectly suited to creepy Jared Wheeler, it's her. What does Darcie even see in these cretins? I clock the darkening expression on Ben's face and climb slowly to my feet, pushing my notebook into my back pocket with the pencil. Ben has never kicked my arse before, but he didn't exactly stop Jared and the others from kicking it, so I am naturally uneasy.

I glance down and see the mist intensifying in colour. It turns from light to dark grey as it spins around my hands, creating cloud-like gloves that no one else can see - except from Darcie. She's staring at my hands like they are something from a horror movie. I shove them into my pockets and attempt to look casual.

'*Really?*' Ben cocks his head to one side and asks. He runs his tongue around the inside of his mouth as his eyes run me up and down. He then spits to one side and fixes his glare on Darcie. 'You've got to be kidding me.'

To her credit, Darcie pulls herself together pretty fast. I like that about her. Me, I'm an emotional mess, but this girl is a class act. She straightens up and slips an arm protectively through mine, while Vicky's mouth drops open in mock horror.

'We're just friends before you do anything stupid,' she tells Ben calmly and clearly. 'JJ has nothing to do with us breaking up so don't even go there, Ben.'

Ben shakes his head and licks his lips. I can tell by his expression that he's trying to work out how to respond without losing any more face. For a moment I feel genuine pity for him. Maybe he really felt something for Darcie.

'Knew you'd been acting shady,' Vicky scathes, stepping forward suddenly, her eyes all lit up with spite. 'First I thought you were after Jared but now it turns out you've been running around behind our backs with *this* freak!'

'Vicky…' Ben puts a hand on her shoulder, but she shakes him off and glares daggers at me.

'JJ is not a freak,' says Darcie, which almost makes me smile, because she more than anyone knows that I actually am. 'We got talking at the river that day. You guys were absolutely vile to him! It's called bullying you know.'

Vicky laughs out loud, actually throwing her head back to really let us know how hilarious she finds this accusation. 'As if!' she yells at Darcie.

Darcie ignores her and turns to Ben. 'We're just friends,' she says again, 'okay? I broke up with you for my own reasons. Don't take it out on JJ.'

We all look at Ben; Darcie and I hoping he listens to her plea and Vicky no doubt hoping for a battle cry. I'm mildly surprised when he steps back, exhaling again and lifting his hands in a gesture of surrender.

'All right,' he says, 'whatever. If you wanna hang around with the weird kid, that's totally up to you. No hard feelings.'

It's kind of an insult but at the same time, he's not punching me in the face or stealing my notebook from me, so I'm okay with it. Darcie's shoulders drop in relief and it looks like everything is maybe going to be all right, when big-mouth Vicky lets rip.

She grabs Ben's arm and yanks him back into place. 'Are you actually gonna let this creep get away with this?' she demands, her face jutting towards his.

Ben rolls his eyes at her. 'Look, Vicky…'

She flings out an arm pointing it my way. 'The kid's a total mental case! And you're letting him steal your girl? Oh my God Ben *seriously*, it's like you *want* people to laugh at you!'

'I don't care, okay?' He pulls his arm away and starts walking. 'They're welcome to each other!'

'We're just friends!' Darcie shouts after him and in response, he shoves his hands into his pockets and walks faster.

'Jesus Christ,' Vicky shakes her head in dismay and watches him go. 'Jared is *not* gonna be happy about this.'

'What's he got to do with anything?' snaps Darcie, her arm slipping from mine as she crosses the bandstand and trots down the steps to face Vicky. 'Who I choose to hang out with in my own time is no one else's business Vicky! Not yours, or Ben's and definitely not Jared's!'

To this, Vicky tilts her head, narrows her eyes, and bites her lower lip. She has the look of someone who is figuring something out and feeling particularly smug about it too.

'Poor Jared though,' she says, rocking back on her heels. 'First he gets battered almost to death in the toilets and then one of his best friends wimps out on him.' She shoots a hard glare my way. 'Ben should've kicked your arse, *creep*!'

'He's not a creep,' says Darcie, gesturing for me to follow. 'And we're out of here. C'mon, JJ.'

I follow, thinking she has the right idea. We need to get as far away from people like Ben and Vicky as possible and added to that, I can feel my hands getting colder in my pockets.

'That was so random though,' Vicky sings out as we pass her. 'No one else was about that night, you know? Just us guys hanging out and then Jared and you both disappear on us, DeeDee?' Vicky shrugs her shoulders as Darcie spins to look at her. 'Just find that kind of weird, that's all. Maybe it's just me. It's not like poor Jared can remember anything. His brain's been messed up, you know. They don't think he'll ever be quite the same. Hell of a thing for someone to live with, isn't it? Just think, DeeDee, there's someone walking around right now who knows it was them and knows they brain damaged another kid. Shit! I think I'd go nuts.'

Darcie holds her ground and I can see the skin on her face trembling as she tries desperately hard to contain herself.

'Let's go, Darcie,' I speak up for the first time and pull my hand out of my pocket to tug at her sleeve. The mist has got darker again - it's almost black, coiling like snakes around my fingers. I drop my hand away from her and close my fist and it feels like crushing ice.

'If you've got something to say, just say it,' Darcie glares at Vicky, resisting my tug on her sleeve.

Vicky takes a step back and gives Darcie the up and down look I'm so used to getting myself. 'Maybe I will,' she responds, 'maybe the police haven't considered everything, you know? I mean, you weren't with us for the time Jared was gone. Maybe I ought to tell them that.'

'Why haven't you told them already?'

'Come on Darcie,' I pull at her arm again. 'Let's just go.'

'How do you know I haven't?' Vicky bellows at her and I can suddenly see this thing turning nasty. Darcie is like a block of stone, standing there so rigid, leaning forward ever so slightly as if poised to attack. And Vicky has such a vicious look in her eyes…

I pull at Darcie's arm harder and manage to move her along. 'Seriously, we need to go. The mist…' I hiss into her ear and she finally looks down. She sees the way it's tightening around my fingers like rope and her eyes grow wider. She nods and lets me pull her on.

'Going so soon?' Vicky asks. 'I thought we were having fun, DeeDee. You know, getting to know each other better. I mean, you're quite the girl of mystery if you think about it.'

'Goodbye Vicky,' Darcie mutters and we stride quickly away.

I pick up the pace and walk faster, suddenly terrified that Vicky will come after us and throw more accusations. I'm worried for Darcie. No one knew I was still in the park the night Jared got hurt, and for all his flaws, Uncle Henry did give me an alibi. But what about Darcie? Christ, none of this is her fault!

'I'm really sorry,' I mutter as we keep walking.

'Don't worry,' she hisses back, 'I don't think she saw it. I think it's just me, JJ.'

'I thought you two were gonna get in a fight…'

She snorts. 'Yeah, I think I was close to be honest. She's such a *bitch*.'

'She knows, Darcie, she knows! She was basically threatening you!'

Darcie takes a deep breath and shakes her head, flicking her ponytail from side to side as if shaking off the whole unpleasant experience. 'She's just having fun,' she says. 'That's her all over. She's just a vindictive little bitch. But I tell you what, we better be careful from now on. I don't want her following us like that again. I've got loads to tell you, JJ! I'm sorry I didn't call when I said I would, but I went down this rabbit hole of research...'

She glances at me and braves a weary smile. I nod back. 'I know a place we can go to talk.'

'Awesome, where?'

'Hangman's Cottage.'

Her mouth falls open and her eyes light up. She jabs me with an elbow. 'There is no such place, JJ Carson!'

'There is,' I nod, grimly. 'I'll show you.'

'It sounds amazing, like something out of a horror movie. Why there?'

I give a small shrug and release a long sigh. 'It's where my mother grew up.'

16: Darcie

I can't believe my eyes as we round the corner along the entrance to the river path.

'Seriously, how have I never heard of this place?'

JJ shrugs, his eyes firmly fixed on the ancient cottage before us. He hops over the little gate and snakes around the back. I stand shivering in the cold for a moment and take in my surroundings. The cottage looks as if it hasn't been lived in for years, its walls moss-ridden and front garden littered with weeds. I place my hands against the chipped paint on the gate and I am shocked by how soft it feels. It's almost as if it could crumble apart at any moment. With caution, I climb over it too, and approach the small wooden door. The cracked paving slabs wobble underfoot and threaten to give way, but I hop onto the filthy welcome mat just in time.

JJ unlocks the door from the inside. You can tell nobody has tried to open it in a while because he really has to pull it several times just to create enough of a gap for me to slip through. My nose wrinkles as the dusty air hits my face. Almost every surface is caked in cobwebs. I feel them stroking my cheeks and clinging to my hair as I creep through the darkness. This place is like a rabbit warren. The living room and kitchen are open plan, but down the hall there are too many doors to count and a set of wooden steps lead up to a second floor. I shudder.

'Hang on,' JJ says from deep inside the gloom. He pulls open a drawer in the kitchen and reveals a box of matches. He strikes one along the edge of the pack, shielding the tiny flame with his hand. 'There should be a candle over there,' he nods to my left. Sure enough, there it is. I pick up the holder, surprised by its weight, and place it down on the kitchen counter.

'But… How did you…?' I ask as he uses the match to light it.

'I used to come here a lot… Sneak in through there.' He glances over his shoulder to a room at the back, and through the open door I can just make out a small square window. I perch on a stool by the counter and JJ slumps into a floral armchair.

'Used to?' I ask him.

He shrugs. 'When I was little. I came back a few times after… after I moved in with Uncle Henry, but he found out and went nuts. He doesn't want me here.'

'Wow,' I breathe, trying to take it all in. 'Are we safe here?'

'Yeah. Nobody ever comes here. People think it's haunted, you know.'

We sit in silence for a while. I know I should tell JJ what I discovered about the mist but looking at him now, I just don't have the heart. His eyes are glazed over, and I can tell he is lost in some distant memory. This place must mean a lot to him.

'So, your mom, she really grew up here?'

'Yeah, with my gran.'

'What about your grandfather?'

'He died when she was eight. Hung himself apparently.'

'Oh shit! I'm sorry.'

JJ shrugs, his eyes don't move from the floor. I get up and walk over to the mantel, there's a row of old photographs in dusty metal frames. I lift one to the light and blow the cobwebs from it.

'All her stuff is still here,' JJ sighs. 'No one's been in here in a while, I guess.' His cheeks grow red as he joins me at the mantel and points at a dusty picture of a middle-aged woman standing behind a little girl. 'That's my mum there in that one, with Grandma.'

'They're both so pretty,' I gasp, staring into their faces. I can see JJ in both of them. For the first time he glances up at me.

There's a world of pain in the eyes of JJ Carson. If you take the time to look at him, and I mean really look at him, you can feel it pulling you in. I place the photograph back on the mantel and we return to our seats.

'Do you want to talk about her… your mom I mean?'

'Not really.'

'How about this place, you said it was called *Hangman's cottage?*'

'It's been around forever. It used to be three, but they knocked down the walls years ago and made it into one.' For a moment he is smiling again, I can tell he likes to talk about this sort of stuff. History. 'Apparently, the executioner used to live here back in the sixteen-hundreds. Fortune's Well was loads better back then.'

'Better?'

His eyes turn dark and he shuffles further back into his chair. 'People were punished when they did something wrong.'

'People like Jared Wheeler you mean?'

'Yeah.'

There's that silence again.

'I'm sorry by the way.'

'For what?'

'For never stopping him sooner. I just, I don't know…'

'It's okay.'

'No. No, JJ, it's not. It's not okay at all. If I had just said something sooner, then maybe, just maybe-'

'Maybe what? I'd be less fucked up?' He laughs and I just stand there not knowing what to say. 'It's fine, Darcie. That prick Jared didn't make me this way.' He glances down at his hands, examining his wrists and flexing his fingers. 'She did.'

'She?'

'My mum.' *So, he does want to talk about her after all.*

'How so?' I ask, slightly afraid of where this is going.

'By what she did to my dad. It's sick, isn't it? I mean, how could she do that? How could she leave me with nobody but bloody Uncle Henry?'

I shift awkwardly, not sure how to steer the conversation back to something lighter.

'And he's just as fucked-up,' JJ continues. 'And my old man, too—cheating on her like that.'

'Is that why she…?'

He clenches his fists tightly and slams them against the arms of the chair. I notice a few grey wisps lingering around the fabric as he pushes himself up and begins pacing around the room. I have to tell him about what I've discovered. I have to tell him now before something else happens and I don't have the chance. Taking a deep breath, I count down in my head. *3… 2… 1…*

'Enenra.'

He is looking at me now like I'm crazy. I rub my hands against my face and start again.

'There's this thing on Jeremy's video game.'

'Video game?' he laughs, and I am happy to see the puffs of mist around his hands begin to fade away. 'What are you talking about?' Then I watch his face grow serious as he realises this is important.

'There are these creatures. Demons, I guess. They feed on human souls. Negative energy. They can look like regular humans just like you and me, but in their truest form, well...' I peer down at his hands and he follows my gaze to the flow of darkness that has begun to wrap around them like a second skin.

'No. That's stupid. It doesn't make any sense. You don't really believe in that sorta stuff, do you?'

'A week ago, I didn't believe teenage boys could have superpowers.'

He grins.

'Do you think maybe we should talk to someone?'

'Like who? A priest?'

'No, like your uncle. I know he's an ass to you sometimes but clearly we need help.'

'No,' JJ growls as he shakes his head firmly at me. 'No way. He'd have me sent straight to the nut house.'

'Well, there has to be someone that knows what's going on with you. How about...'
I stop myself.

'How about, what?'

I take a breath. 'How about your mom?'

He jumps backwards, shaking his hands at me. 'No, no, no. No way. I can't talk to her right now, I just can't. Besides, I'm not allowed Darcie. Uncle Henry won't let me!'

The mist around his hands intensifies. It's moving along his arms and up to his shoulders. He notices too and the more he panics, the more it spreads. It coils around his neck like a noose. Growing thicker. Tighter. He begins to choke, and I dart forwards, trying with all my might to pull it away from him but I can't, my fingers just slip right through. He begins to shiver, and his skin adopts a blueish tinge. I keep clawing away even though I know that there is nothing I can do to save him.

'Fight it, JJ! You have to fight it!'

His body convulses but I can tell that he can hear me, and he is doing his best to break free. I grab hold of his hand and squeeze it tightly. His skin is so cold that I can feel the ache throbbing in my own fingers. 'Please, JJ. Don't let it take you.'

With one last shudder its grip on him shatters and I watch, open-mouthed, as it fizzles away in mid-air until it's as if it was never even there at all. I fling my arms around his shoulders and pull him into a hug. He's shivering, so I grab a blanket from the floor and drape it around him. A red blot splashes against it. Then another. And another.

'You're bleeding.'

He wipes a hand across his nostrils and more blood begins to roll down his chin.

'Shit.' He pinches the bridge of his nose and catches the flow with his other hand. I run across to the kitchen and search through the cabinet for something to soak up the blood. No use.

'Bathroom?'

'Down the hall,' he winces, nodding towards the room at the back with the little window.

Inside, I find nothing but a few empty pill bottles and an old hand towel slung over the edge of sink; it looks pretty filthy but it's the best option we have. I shake it off and try the tap. *Great, no water.* As I glance up into the mirror, I feel all the blood in my own body sink straight to my feet. In the reflection I can see the lounge from where I came. I can see the floral armchair, where JJ Carson is sat hunched forward holding his nose. I can also see the huge black shadow that's looming behind him. It peers down at him, dark robes hiding its face, axe in hand.

Hangman.

I dig my fingernails into the edge of the sink and scream.

17: JJ

Jesus Christ… Darcie's scream is enough to wake the dead, let alone the whole bloody town. It's a good thing Hangman's Cottage doesn't have any close neighbours, or someone would be calling the police on us right now.

I jerk upright in the chair, struggling to turn both ways with the blanket around my shoulders. Her hand is raised, and she is pointing behind me. 'What?' I almost scream, because although there is blatantly nothing there, the look on her face tells me otherwise. She has gone so pale it looks like the blood has just leached out of her.

'Behind you,' Darcie says, and her voice is just a croak, almost inaudible as her hands meet her face and she covers her mouth as if to hold in another shriek.

I force myself to my feet, which is a bad move because the floor sways and the walls move and more blood rolls from my nostrils and spatters on to the armchair. There is nothing behind me except a shadowy bookcase smothered by cobwebs. I suddenly feel Darcie's fingers sink into my shoulder and I yelp in pain. She gets a good grip on me and starts pulling me backwards, never taking her eyes from whatever it is she can see.

'There's nothing there, Darcie,' I tell her gently, as we move out of the room and back into the hallway. 'What's wrong with you?'

'There was someone behind you,' she replies, her voice a sob-choked breath against my neck. She keeps moving backwards, carefully but quickly, until her back hits the front door and she scrambles for a hold of the doorknob.

'Darcie…'

'I'm *serious*,' she whispers and now I can feel her tears, so warm against my cold skin, as she rests her chin on my shoulder and stares into the darkness. Behind her she frantically works the doorknob until the door gives way and a blast of warm summer air washes over us.

'Darcie, come on.'

'I'm not kidding,' she repeats firmly, and although she is most definitely crying, Darcie also sounds as serious as hell. She kicks the door open with the heel of one foot and drags me outside with her.

I turn to face her, still wiping away blood and with the musty old blanket still around my shoulders. Somewhere in the trees a tawny owl hoots, making us both jump as it sounds so close. Darcie reaches around me and slams the door shut, her eyes wide and her lips pulled back from her teeth in distaste.

'What the hell?' I look at her and shake my head. 'Darcie? Hey?'

But she doesn't look at me, she just stumbles over to the low stone wall and sits down fast, her knees spread open as she rests her elbows on them and drops her face dramatically into her hands.

'Darcie?' I drop the blanket and join her on the wall. My nose releases two more fat drops of blood onto the scrubby ground and then stops. Just like that. I sit for a moment and just stare at the cottage. It looks fat and squat and foreboding in the moonlight and shadows. Nothing like the quaint cottage my grandmother and mother both grew up in. Back then the front garden was full of roses and twisting honeysuckle. My grandmother kept chickens and ducks who would follow me around when I was little, waiting for me to drop crumbs.

'What the hell is wrong with us?' Darcie moans softly beside me and when I look at her, I cannot stop myself placing an arm around her shoulders and pulling her into me.

'It's okay,' I tell her, but we both know it isn't. We both know it is very far from okay. Thinking about everything that has happened, I almost want to laugh. I squeeze against her and rub my hand up and down her arm. 'Actually, it's really not okay, is it?' I say and she releases a snort of laughter before shaking her head. 'It's all mental,' I add. 'I bet you wish you'd never stopped to help me that day at the river. It's like we've both been cursed since then, I swear.'

She snorts again then drops her hands and looks right at me. 'JJ, when did you first start seeing the mist? I mean, can you remember how old you were when you started seeing it in your drawings?'

I bite my lower lip for a moment, considering the question. 'Ah, I dunno…probably, maybe it was after my mum went to prison so I would have been ten, I guess. But it was… I dunno, not that obvious.'

'Not like it is now?' she prompts.

I shake my head firmly. 'No way. It was fainter. It was nothing really. For ages I just thought I was imagining it. My mum always said I had a vivid imagination you know. Like her.'

Darcie sniffs and uses the back of her hand to wipe away her tears. She is still shaking so I keep holding her close.

'When did it happen? When did it appear?'

'I dunno,' I shrug. 'Random times.'

'When you were sad or angry?'

102

'I don't know, Darcie. Why are you asking? Are you gonna tell me what the hell that was all about in there just now?'

She holds up a hand and takes a deep breath, steadying herself. 'Hang on. One thing at a time, JJ, I need to figure this out. *We* need to figure all of this out or seriously, we're both gonna go crazy.'

'Okay,' I nod at her. 'Okay then.'

'Did the mist ever appear when you were happy?'

Now it's my turn to snort laughter. 'Happy? I don't think I've been happy since I moved here, Darcie.'

'Okay,' she nods, wiping at her eyes again before smoothing back her hair. 'So, it would only appear when you were sad or angry or alone…'

'Yeah, I guess, but I don't know what that's got to do with anything or with what you saw in there? What was it, Darcie? You're still pale. Like you've seen a ghost.'

'I thought I saw my Aunt Jenna once,' she says then, her gaze fixed on the cottage as her eyes shine with unshed tears. 'After she died.'

'Really? Like a ghost you mean?'

'She was across the street back home,' Darcie goes on, 'just watching me and smiling. I literally blinked and then she was gone. I told my parents about it obviously, but they just thought it was, you know, a typical Darcie thing to say. Aunt Jenna was super sensitive, they always said, whatever the hell that means. They'd say I was the same…' She drifts off for a moment, her brow creased in confusion as she attempts to figure it all out. I realise then that it's one of the things I most like about her. She might be scared or angry or sad, but she doesn't ever let that stop her, she just keeps going, keeps trying to figure things out.

I sigh gently and rest my head against hers. I suddenly feel safer and happier than I have done in years, and it's nice. Really nice.

'I saw her here too,' Darcie says then after clearing her throat. 'Not long after we arrived, I thought I saw her watching me at school.'

'Do you believe in ghosts?' I ask her.

She folds her arms over her chest and rubs away the chill. 'I do now,' she says, grimly. 'JJ, I don't know what to think - not about anything. I feel like me and you are mixed up in something that no one else can see or understand, or would ever believe, but it's happening, right? We're not crazy, are we?'

Her eyes shift from the cottage finally and meet mine. I swallow nervously, fighting the urge to reach out and stroke her cheek. 'I don't know about me, but I'm sure you're not crazy, Darcie. But please tell me, what did you see in there?'

'Besides the black mist that was full on strangling you?' she asks, neat eyebrows raised. I nod in reply and she takes a deep breath. 'As if that wasn't bad enough,' she murmurs, 'when I looked back at you, I could see a dark figure standing behind you. Over you. He had an axe or something like that, I swear. He was holding something heavy.'

'Okay, okay, on any other day I'd say you were imagining it, but I just got strangled by black mist I create myself, so, you know...' I laugh a little and shrug at her. 'I'm gonna go with believing you instantly on this.'

'I think it was the Hangman,' she adds, staring reluctantly at the cottage. 'And JJ, I would really, really like to get the hell away from this place right now.'

'No problem.' I get up and she follows. 'Where to? I don't think Uncle Henry wants me home for a while. He's entertaining the waitress again.'

Darcie frowns at me. 'I called your house earlier and he said you smashed up a TV?'

'Uh *shit*, I forgot about that,' I groan as we pick our way back down to the river path. 'Oh Christ, he's gonna kill me.'

'Why'd you smash it?'

'Because he pissed me off. Long story. After he left, I just picked it up and threw it.'

Darcie reaches out and grabs my hand to slow me down. 'Mist?' she asks, knowingly.

'Yeah,' I agree. 'Mist.'

'This is serious, JJ. How does it work? Are you in control of it? Can you make it come? Did it help you beat Jared like that?'

'I think so,' I shrug at her as we head down the dark wooded path. 'It's like it takes over or something. Darcie? Where the hell are we going?'

She stops and thinks for a moment and then her eyes brighten, and she smiles. 'My house,' she says. 'I want to introduce you to my parents.'

18: Darcie

He looks at me like I'm joking and to be honest I don't blame him. I mean, what on earth am I thinking? Bringing him back to my place… My mother will eat him alive. But what other option do we have? I can tell that JJ wants to be anywhere but home right now and I can't risk leaving him on his own. Besides, my mother can't be any scarier than whatever strange apparition I just saw… *Can she?*

When we make it to the door my hand rests on the handle for a split second. Before I am able to talk myself out of it, Jeremy yanks it open from the other side. He's dressed in checked pyjama bottoms and an oversized Simpsons t-shirt.

'You're back. I've unlocked a new costume for-' He stops when he notices JJ shifting awkwardly at the bottom of the steps. 'Oh, hi.'

'Jer, JJ—JJ, Jer,' I grin. My brother nods then moves towards the stairs. *Poor Jeremy… I wonder what's been going on with him lately. He's definitely been quieter than usual.* I step inside and hold the door for JJ, who climbs the steps cautiously and leans against the doorframe.

'You're not a vampire, I don't need to invite you in,' I laugh. He smiles back at me and steps into the light of the hallway. Shrugging out of my jacket I sling it over the banister and take hold of his arm, leading him through to the kitchen.

'C'mon, let's get you something to eat.'

He takes a seat at the counter and drums his fingers against the marble surface, as I raid the fridge for leftovers. I grab a plate from the cupboard and begin to pile it high, placing it in front of him with a smile. 'Bon appétit!' I pour myself a glass of water and lean my back against the sink, observing him. I can't help but smile as he pushes around the strange green substance with his fork.

'Erm, what's this?'

'Your guess is as good as mine.'

My mother appears from the lounge. She's still dressed to the nines from dinner earlier and I can't help but notice her eyes widen as she approaches the wine rack. 'Oh, sweetheart, who do we have here?' She flashes a smile as she reaches for a bottle, her eyes scanning JJ up and down. He jumps to his feet and rubs his hand against his jeans before thrusting it out to her.

'JJ Carson. Nice to meet you Mrs Duffield.'

She stares down at his hand and back across at me. 'Little late, isn't it?'

'Manners, Mom.' I roll my eyes and join my friend at the counter, placing an arm around his shoulders. 'You remember JJ, don't you? Mr Carson's nephew.' Something strange happens to her then, something I've never thought possible. Her face softens and she takes a seat opposite us, grinning from ear to ear.

'Oh, so you're the young man who lives with Henry.' She fumbles with the cap on the bottle and I walk around to remove it for her. 'Tell me, how is your uncle doing?'

'Erm, fine. I think.'

'Good, good. Farm running smoothly?'

'I suppose so.'

'And what exactly is it *you* do there?'

'Mostly I muck out the barn.'

My mother winces ever so slightly, checks the name on the bottle, then composes herself. 'Bit sweet,' she lies. But I know the truth of course; she couldn't ever imagine doing such filthy work herself. I admire JJ for it though. He is a hard-working kid despite all the shit he has to contend with. Literally. If I had just a fraction of his strength, goodness knows I'd be happy with that. I take a long gulp of water as he rocks back and forth on the stool not knowing what to say. My mother rotates the glass in her hand admiring its contents.

'So, JJ,' she pauses for a second. 'I don't mean to pry, but do you get to see your mother at all?'

'Okay, Mom. This has been great, but JJ needs to eat,' I grab him by the arm and pull him to his feet. He looks down at the green mixture and frowns. I throw him a look and he reluctantly picks up the plate. My mother shrugs and takes a long sip of wine. We head up the stairs to my room, I take the plate from him and place it on my desk. From my drawer I remove two breakfast bars and toss them towards him.

'Thanks,' he grins, tearing open the wrappers so fast that if I'd blink, I'd have missed it. I gesture for him to take a seat on the bed whilst I perch on the swivel chair at the desk. 'So,' he says amidst chews, 'you wanna talk about that thing you saw?'

'He was stood right there, leaning over you. Just watching.' I shudder as I relive the memory. 'He was a bit hazy, kinda like your mist, but he was definitely there… JJ, are you sure you didn't see anything?'

'Nothing.'

I bite my lip and swing the chair from left to right with my feet. He reaches into his pocket and withdraws his sketch pad and pencil. 'Why don't I draw what you say you saw?'

I smile back at him. 'We're just like real detectives now, aren't we?'

'We can even have code names if you want?'

'Hmm, how about *Disaster Girl and Misty*?'

'Sounds like a kid's show.' He laughs, and it's a great sound. It starts something inside of me that I can't quite explain. I begin to describe the image and his hand darts excitedly across the page. Moments later he has finished. He turns the pad to face me and I'm shocked. Staring right back at me is an exact replica of the Hangman. I can't help but gasp. It's so much like him that it is as if it were a photograph, I can almost imagine him climbing out of the page and filling up my room—trapping us. I nod towards JJ, confirming that the likeness is uncanny, then move across to sit next to him on the bed.

'Please don't get upset again,' I ask, placing a hand on his. 'But I'm really worried about you.'

'I know.'

'If what I read before has any truth to it—whatever this *mist* is—it could kill you, JJ. I think after tonight you must know that.' He nods and peers across at the framed photograph by the bed. He lifts it up and examines it.

'Is this-'

'Aunt Jenna. Yeah.' I take the frame from him and stare into her bright blue eyes.

'She's pretty.'

'Yeah. This was taken on my birthday. Mom and Dad said I couldn't eat too much sugar, but Jenna snuck me and Jeremy out for ice cream.' I smile and run a finger across her face. Tears begin to fill my eyes and roll down my cheeks. I wipe them away with my sleeve. 'I hate that she's gone. I hate it every day. I can't let this be you too, JJ. You're the first real friend I've had.'

He squeezes my hand and turns to face me. 'I'm sorry for how I acted back at the cottage,' he says, his face inching closer. 'I think you were right though. I think I should go and see my mum. I'm just not sure if I can do it... Not yet anyway. But if she really has the answers, I guess I'll have to try. You're never gonna lose me, Darcie.'

Our foreheads are touching now, and my heart begins to race. JJ holds steady, I can feel his warm breath against my face. There's something like static between us. Just one more movement, just one, and our lips will meet. I hesitate, counting down in my mind.

3...

2...

There's a creak from one of the floorboards in the hallway and we break apart. He sweeps the hair from his face and I continue to examine the photograph of Jenna. In the doorway, my dad emerges. He leans up against the wall with his arms folded, eyebrows raised and a teasing smile painting his face.

'I thought I heard voices.'

'Dad, this is JJ-'

'Carson. Your mother told me.'

'Nice to meet you, sir.' JJ rises from the bed and unlike my mother, my dad reaches forward and shakes his proffered hand.

'Listen, sweetie, it's late. I'm sure Mr Carson will be wondering where his nephew is.'

JJ shoots me a look and I try to suppress a smile.

'You're right,' JJ says, collecting his sketch pad and pencil from the bed. I notice my dad shoot a quick glance at the drawing before he flips it shut. 'I better start heading back.'

'Woah, woah, woah. Hold on, young man. I'll drive you home. Can't allow you to walk the streets alone at night.' He places a hand on JJ's shoulder. 'Who knows what terrible things are lurking in the dark.'

JJ agrees, flashes me a grin and then disappears out into the hallway. I rise from the bed and grab hold of my dad's arm. 'He's a good guy, Dad.'

'I'm sure he is.'

'Just don't give him the third degree.'

'Oh, honey, what kind of father would I be if I found a stranger in my daughter's room and didn't interrogate him just a little.' He smiles then notes my worried expression. 'Relax, it's just a ride home.'

He pulls me against him and kisses my forehead, then takes the photograph from my hand. 'You know, you and your aunt Jenna are like two peas in a pod.' I look up at him and smile. It has been ages since I heard anyone in my family mention her name. I'm not even sure if Jeremy even remembers who she is.

'So damn sensitive,' he concludes, smiling.

I grin up at him and he pulls away, placing the photograph back by the bed. I notice something in his eyes change as he examines it one last time. Inside, my head is screaming out for me to ask him more questions about her. Does he miss her as much as I do? What is his favourite memory? Why can't we go and visit her grave someday? But nothing leaves my lips. Instead, I simply sink back onto the bed and sigh as he closes the door behind him.

19: JJ

Well, this is awkward…

I'm out of practice talking to adults, talking to anyone. And now here I am stuck in a posh car with Darcie's highly intimidating dad. He keeps smiling at me too. I don't know what to make of it. Is it a genuinely friendly smile? Or is it more like the smile of a shark that wants to eat me? I don't think I impressed Darcie's mother very much, though she lit up a bit when Uncle Henry was mentioned. All the women like Uncle Henry and he knows it.

'So, how long have you and Darcie been friends?' Mr Duffield asks me as he drives the car out of their vast driveway.

Shit, I don't even know…

'Um, not long,' I stutter, sounding like an imbecile. 'I mean, I've seen her at school, but I only started talking to her recently.'

'Oh?' he looks at me again, taking his eyes off the road for just a tad too long, if I'm honest. 'Why was that?'

'Um… I, well…' Shit, shit, I have no idea, I literally have no words! 'Uh…' I shake my hair back, glance out of the window and then come up with something. 'She kind of helped me out one day. Stood up for me with these kids that had been giving me a hard time.'

It's basically the truth but I'm not sure how I'll respond if Mr Duffield wants to know the kid's names.

'I see,' his eyes are on me again, and there is that eerie smile too. 'Well, that sounds just like Darcie, to me. She's always had a social conscience, that girl. Always looking out for others.' He glances at the road only briefly before his gaze lands on me again. 'She's got a very pure heart, my daughter.'

'Oh yeah,' I say, clumsily, staring at my hands on my lap and wondering what to do with them. A sudden panic seizes me - what if the mist starts up again? Jesus, what if it attacks me again? He'll just see this crazy boy squirming around in his car, grabbing at his own neck... Oh my God, please no. 'Uh, she really does.'

'I hope you don't mind me saying,' Mr Duffield looks back at the road for a change, which is a relief in more ways than one. 'And please tell me to mind my own business if I'm stepping out of line here, JJ, but you know, this is a *very* small town. One of the reasons we moved here actually. It's just so quaint, so English. And we really wanted to live somewhere where everyone knew each other, you know?' He shoots me a look, so I nod quickly and firmly and thankfully his eyes return to the road in front. 'Funnily enough, I actually have some very distant ancestors that came from here, did you know that?'

I look at him and he's looking back at me again, his eyes all wide and eager, and I really can't work him out. He's more than a little bit odd. 'Oh, really?' I ask, feigning interest. 'That's awesome.'

'Generations ago,' he adds, 'but anyway, obviously I heard about your situation. About your mother and father and your uncle stepping in to give you a home. I'm sorry JJ, that is a hell of a lot for a young man to go through.'

His eyes are on me again, so I nod my head. 'Thanks.'

'Your mother, she was born in Fortune's Well like your father?'

Why does he care? I sigh and nod. 'Yep.'

'They must have been childhood sweethearts?'

'Something like that,' I gaze out of the window and try to determine how close to the farm we are.

'And how is she doing, if you don't mind me asking? Your mother.'

Jesus…

'Um, I don't know, okay I guess,' I offer a shrug as his eyes meet mine for a long, drawn out moment. How can he drive like that? It's like he knows the roads like the back of his hand. 'My uncle doesn't like me seeing her,' I add then, because Mr Duffield is still staring at me.

He smiles. 'I'm sorry to hear that. You'd like to see her though?'

'Yeah,' I nod. 'I kind of need to right now.'

'I can imagine,' he says softly. 'Well, we are nearly there, JJ. I could always come to the door, maybe have a little word with your uncle for you? Or would that be treading on toes?' He looks at me then laughs. 'Oh yes, I can tell by the look on your face that it is. You'll have to excuse this brash and obnoxious American, JJ. It'll take me some time to get used to how reserved the English are!'

'It's okay. Thanks for the lift.'

He pulls into the farmyard and puts the handbrake on. 'You're very welcome, young man. I'm so glad my daughter was there for you when you needed it. You know, you'll find you have a friend for life in that one, if you let her.'

What do I even say to that? I'm pretty sure Darcie and I almost kissed earlier. I don't think Mr Duffield would be so friendly if he knew about that. I just smile my fake smile and climb out of the car.

'Thank you, Mr Duffield.'

'No problem!' He lifts a hand in a cheery wave, I close the door and he swerves to the right, makes a tight circle and drives out of the yard with a spray of gravel behind him.

Holy shit, that was possibly the most awkward car drive of my life.

And now I have to face Uncle Henry.

I trudge wearily up to the front door. I feel exhausted. The confrontation with Ben and Vicky, the cottage, the mist, the hangman - it's been one hell of a night. I just want to get to my room and hit the pillow hard.

But when I open the door he's there. He's sprawled on the sofa in just a pair of white boxers. He's smoking a cigarette and looks close to falling asleep. The smashed TV is upright and I gulp nervously looking at it as I close the front door behind me. Uncle Henry has the waitress entwined with his body; her long limbs woven through his, which is probably a good thing. If he tries to get me, he'll trip up over her and hit the floor first.

'I'm sorry about the TV,' I say before he can. I hold up my hands in surrender because he sure doesn't tolerate a smart arse or a rebel. I edge around the room, keeping my eyes on him, hoping he is too drunk and too tired to bother with a fight.

'What the hell happened?' he mumbles, his voice slurred. He twists to see me as I head for the hall and his movements disturb the waitress, who lifts her head, groans and then tumbles from his lap. He stares at her for a moment in surprise and when she doesn't move, he gets up and steps over her.

Shit.

'I just knocked it,' I say, backing up, smiling weakly. 'I was banging the hoover around, you know, too fast, I'm sorry, and I turned and just bashed into it and it fell. I'll pay for it. I mean, I'll work it off. Whatever you want.'

115

He pauses in the hallway, leaning heavily on the wall. 'Don't matter,' he says, eyebrows raised. 'Nothing but shit on anyway.'

I risk a smile. 'Okay.'

'Where you been?'

'I met up with Darcie. We hung out for a bit. Ended up at her house then her dad drove me home.' I nod at him as he frowns.

'Oh yeah? Her old man drove you home, eh?'

'Yep. He seems nice.'

'So, what? You and her are...? What?'

'Nothing,' I say, shaking my head. 'Just friends. I barely know her. She was just good to me, she helped me out, that's all.'

'Interesting,' he says watching me as he strokes his chin. 'You've finally made a friend then? After all these years? Maybe you're not so much the odd kid anymore, eh?'

Odd kid?

I just smile at him. 'Maybe. Darcie is really nice. I'm glad we're friends.' I want to add that she's good for me, but I don't. I just want to go to bed.

But Uncle Henry staggers forward, reaching for me. I back up a little, but I don't want to piss him off, so I stop when I reach the bottom stair and his heavy hands land on my shoulders, pressing me down. He leans into me and his hot breath reeks of beer and cigarettes.

A silly smile pulls at his lips 'You're not so bad,' he tells me, and his left hand moves up to the back of my neck in a gesture that reminds me of my dad. My dad, his warm rough hand cupping the back of my neck on a summer's day in our back garden, far from here, when we had a life. When we had a family. I gaze at the floor and just nod. Henry ruffles my hair with his other hand and lets out a little chuckle. 'You not so bad…' he goes on, 'you trying, aren't you? Eh? You trying not to be like her? I know you are, I *know* you are. You're always trying.'

'Okay,' I say because I don't know what the hell else to say. 'Thanks Uncle Henry, I really got to get to bed now so…'

'Okay, okay,' he says, letting me go and straightening up. 'You go bed. I got to finish the waitress anyway!' He grins wildly and winks at me. 'You go to bed, JJ but I just want you to know…I just want you to know why you can't see her no more, okay?' His eyes are dark and solemn as he leans back against the wall and points at me. 'I'm not being the bad guy, I don't wanna always be the bad guy, JJ, but I got to be, *someone* got to be! Someone got to make sure you don't turn out like her or her mother!'

I want to ask him about that, but I can't, not now and not while he's like this. So, I just nod and smile like I'm ever so grateful to him for stopping me seeing my mother in prison. I nod in understanding and wave goodnight and back up the stairs with a tight smile on my face. And Uncle Henry just watches me go.

In my room, I fall on the bed and don't even bother undressing. I tug my notebook from my pocket and flip open the picture I drew at Darcie's house. It instantly makes me feel cold, inside and out. I stare at it for a second longer before throwing the book on the floor and pulling the duvet tightly over my head. I'm so desperate for sleep but it doesn't come easy. I can't shake the feeling that the hangman is still with me.

20: Darcie

I'm in bed, lost in a memory where the sun burns down brightly on Crescent Bay.

I lift my face towards it and let it stroke my cheeks, warming me. I have to close my eyes, of course; the light makes me see coloured spots and tickles my nose which makes me want to sneeze. I can hear the ocean yawning as it washes up onto the sand beneath my feet. I feel it splash against my toes, and it's just as warm as the sun from above. I smile. The best thing about living in Laguna Beach is being by the ocean. The breeze is fresh and clean, and everything seems so peaceful. I walk out into the sea and I just keep going. I think that when I die, this is the place I'll come to. I heard once in Philosophy class that some old wise guy believed that when you die, your soul returns to its true home. A place more beautiful than anyone can ever imagine. But I refuse to believe there is any place more magical than it is right here in Crescent Bay.

'Darcie, looks who's here!'

My dad's voice dances on the waves from somewhere along the shoreline. I ignore him for a moment, mesmerised by the crystal water surrounding me. Then I hear my brother, Jeremy, scream out excitedly and I know that if I turn, she'll be here. Sure enough, there she is. White shorts, blue bikini top, golden hair billowing around her: Aunt Jenna. I almost cry when I see her. I fight my way back to dry land and I run, and I run, and I - Wow - The warmth of the sunlight and the sea combined is nothing compared to the warmth of her embrace. I never, ever want to let her go. She's laughing at something she said against my ear, but I missed it. My mind is too busy trying to come to terms with the fact that she is actually here, she's real and she's come back to me.

'Whoa, whoa, whoa, kids. Come on. Let your Aunt Jenna breathe.'

'Oh, stop!' she says, slapping a hand against my dad's arm. 'I've been thinking about these hugs the whole way up here.'

'How was the journey?'

'Great! Mom says hi by the way.'

'You saw Grandma Mimi?' my brother asks.

'Sure did.' She sweeps him up into her arms and I feel a little jealous that I'm now far too tall for piggyback rides. 'I stopped by San Diego on my way from Arizona.'

'Oh, how is the *bohemian* lifestyle treating you?' my mother asks. She is hidden behind heavy sunglasses, a humungous floppy hat and a large glass of something French.

'Great thanks, Alice. How's blowing all my brother's cash?'

My mom peers up from her wine with raised eyebrows, then takes a long gulp. Dad shoots Jenna a warning look but she just laughs and rolls her eyes.

'She doesn't mean that Alyssa. Do you, Jen?' Dad scolds, but she's already blocked him out. All her attention now on me and Jeremy.

'So, have you guys missed me, or what?'

We beam up at her, then charge with such force that all three of us topple to the sand.

The memory shifts from that day on the beach and into the next evening. This time I'm wrapped up in the duvet as evening rolls out over Orange County, unable to sleep due to the days' excitement. Today was my birthday and Jenna snuck me and Jeremy out for ice cream. Mom would absolutely flip if she knew just how many scoops I had. I reach under the bed and pull out the small box of treasures Jenna has given me over the years. It rattles as I drag it across the rug then lift it with all my might up onto the mattress. I wrench open the lid and pull out this year's gift: a miniature lighthouse. I wind the key on the back and watch in awe as the light slowly rotates and a gentle tune plays. *Jenna always gives me the best gifts.*

Then, a noise from downstairs steals my focus, it sounds like my dad. His voice is raised, and I can hear the heavy stomping of his feet coming up the stairs towards my room. My heartbeat quickens. *Have I done something wrong? Did Jeremy spill the beans about our outing with Jenna?* There's another voice now, high and desperate. The footsteps have stopped. I slip out of bed and creep over to the door, slowly turning the handle and pulling it open, careful not to make a sound. I hear the second voice again; it sounds a lot like Aunt Jenna's. She is screaming the same thing over and over.

'I won't let them, Malcolm! I don't give a rat's ass! Let me see her!'

There're more footsteps. A scuffle.

'You can't do this!' My dad booms.

'Get. Your. Hands. Off. Me. Ugh! You have no right to keep me from her!'

'She's *my* daughter, Jenna!'

'Which is exactly why I'd expect you to understand!'

I yank the handle and nervously creep across to the top of the stairs. I must have made more noise than I intended because as I peer down, I see my dad staring up at me, holding a squirming Aunt Jenna by the arm. Her eyes widen when she sees me, but he places a hand over her mouth.

'Go back to bed, sweetie. Your Aunt Jenna's just had too much to drink.'

'But-'

'Bed. Now. I'll be up to see you in a minute, 'kay?'

My eyes shift towards Jenna, she's staring up at me and desperately trying to break free. But what can I do? I'm only a girl. Reluctantly, I obey my dad's wishes and run back to the safety of my room. I crouch down by the door with my head against the wall, listening to the muffled voices and clattering until my eyes grow heavy.

*

As the memories of life back home begin to fade, the lighthouse on my bedside table plays the last few chimes and the light stops spinning around the room. I sit upright on the bed and run my hands through my hair. I wish I had the courage to ask my dad about her earlier. Perhaps he could explain that evening to me. He has never talked about it—Not once. I know Aunt Jenna had her share of demons, but there was something in her eyes that night, something wild and desperate.

There's a noise from outside, and my room is suddenly filled with bright yellow. Tossing back the duvet I creep over to the window. I hear the slamming of a car door, followed by a muffled voice. It's my dad. He sounds angry, just like he had all those years ago. I duck behind the curtain and peer out into the drive. There he is, pacing back and forth on his phone. A quick glance at the alarm clock confirms it's 4am. I'd fallen asleep after he left with JJ, but that was hours ago now. *Where the hell has he been?*

He turns his face up to the window and I dart back behind the safety of the curtain. My heart is thumping in my chest. *Did he see me?* I gather the courage to check and when I do, he is back to arguing with the person on the other end of the call, leaning up against his car with his free hand to his forehead. I watch a while longer, straining to get any snippet of conversation I can but it's no use. Eventually he hangs up, peers around the empty drive, back up to my window and disappears out of view. Moments later I hear the slow *stomp, stomp, stomp* of footsteps coming towards my room. I run for the bed and bury myself beneath the covers.

The handle turns and in he walks, my dad; he stands there in the doorway for a moment, breathing. Then I feel him moving closer. I clench my eyes tighter and feign sleep, worried that he'll be mad at me for eavesdropping on his conversation. Then I hear a soft scrape as he picks up the lighthouse, and the clicking sound it makes as he slowly winds the key. Placing it back down, he lets out a heavy sigh before retreating back into the hall. The room is filled with the twinkling melody and I roll over to face the door, waiting for the last of his footsteps to fade. As the light swings around the walls, I spot the girl in the mirror staring at me from across the way. As the glare bounces off her shiny surface, I can't help but notice her wide blue eyes— she looks absolutely terrified.

21: JJ

Strange and disturbing dreams fragment my sleep. I seem to be constantly waking in a sweat from one dream only to tumble right into another. My eyes open to bright sunlight when I hear my bedroom door crash open and suddenly Uncle Henry is looming over my bed. For a moment, my body reacts as if tangled in another nightmare. I feel this overwhelming rage rush through me, and my hands shoot out from under the duvet, a stream of dark grey mist spiralling from my fingers and coating my wrists.

Uncle Henry jerks back, frowning and I sit up straight and shove my hands back under the duvet. For a second there, I think I came really close to grabbing him around the neck. Perhaps sensing this, he keeps his distance, one hand on his hip, the other raking back through his messy hair. He looks like shit - hungover.

'Wakey wakey, lazy-arse,' he grumbles, rubbing at his eye. 'You know we don't have time for lie-ins around here. Is the alarm on your phone broken or what?'

I grab my phone from under my pillow. It's 7am. All the other teenagers in the world are still asleep right now. I feel that rush again and its disarming in its intensity, shooting up from my guts and making my hands tingle like they itch to destroy. I have to fight really hard not to scream in his face.

It's weird. I don't feel like me…

'Sorry,' I mumble, shaking my head slightly as I swing my legs out of bed. Uncle Henry grunts and turns to the door.

'I gotta take the waitress home so when you've done your chores can you tidy up the mess downstairs? I'll be back in a few hours.'

Mess downstairs? The mess *they* made? I can't look at him because I am suddenly so enraged. I want to leap up and shove him in his stupid muscly chest. I want to take a swing at him and see what happens.

'Something wrong?' he snaps at me and I realise I have barely looked at him since he walked in. I don't think I can.

'All right,' I mutter. 'But the waitress? She must have a name, yeah.'

Uncle Henry turns to glare at me. 'What did you say?'

'Nothing. Forget it. I just wondered what her name was.' *And why you never call her it, or call any of them by their names, and why there has to be a different woman every week and a messed-up house that I have to clean up or get yelled at, just for being alive…*

Now he's pointing a finger at me. 'Her name is none of your goddamn business. Get a move on. I've had enough of your shit lately.'

'There's an easy way to solve that.'

Shit! Why did I say that? What the hell is wrong with me this morning? I stare at my hands because they are still tingling… It's like electricity, like something inside me thrumming its way to the surface. My head is overrun with everything Uncle Henry has ever done or said to me that was cruel and unfair and every time, *every time* I let him get away with it, *I* apologised to *him*!

And I try like hell to push these things away, to forget them and brush them aside and for Christ's sake, not let them get to me now! Not now! Not now when my hands

124

are spinning with the dark mist and I can feel the cold spreading down my arms.

'Oh, you've got a mouth on you this morning!' Uncle Henry yells then, facing me with red cheeks and wild eyes. 'What the hell is your problem, JJ? Smashing the TV up wasn't enough for you?'

'That was an accident,' I grunt, snatching yesterday's t-shirt from the floor and yanking it over my head. 'And I just meant…you know… you don't *have* to give me a roof and all that.'

'I don't have to give you a roof?'

I grab my jeans and start pulling them on in a hurry. I need to diffuse this quickly but at the same time, I don't want to. I *want* to argue with him. I want to answer him back. I want him, just for once, to know how he makes me feel.

'You don't have to,' I repeat, and my voice sounds snappy. I don't want it to. Or do I?

Uncle Henry comes closer. His eyes are narrowed in distaste and his breath is coming hard through his flared nostrils as his lips purse tightly together.

'You don't have to,' I say again, straightening up, brushing back my hair and looking him right in the eye. 'That's what I mean. I can go, Uncle Henry. Any time you want. Just say the word and I'll get out of your hair. That's what you want, right?'

I swallow hard, staring back at him, half of me longing for him to snarl and shove me so I can fight him back and do to him what I did to Jared, and half of me longing for him to say sorry, for him to hug or pat me clumsily like last night. He was so different last night…

'There's a lot of things I want, JJ,' he says then, his voice soft.

'You don't want me here,' I state.

He looks me up and down slowly. 'You're an ungrateful little son-of-a-bitch.'

'I'm not,' I reply. 'I'm grateful you took me in, Uncle Henry, I really am. I don't know where I would've gone otherwise. But I don't want to be where I'm not wanted, that's what I'm saying, and I feel most days like you don't want me.'

There. I've said it. *Shit, shit, shit.*

I glance at the mist and it's faded. I look back at Uncle Henry and something cold and hard has settled on to his face.

'You're right,' he says then, stepping closer. 'I don't want you here. I never did.'

I nod back at him. It's not like I didn't know but it still feels like he's shoved a knife into my guts and twisted it. I blink back tears and wait for the rest and already I can feel my hands getting cold again.

'You look just like her for one thing!' he shouts suddenly, making me flinch. 'You don't look like your dad, do you, eh? You look like *her*! Your crazy murdering *bitch* of a mother!'

I nod again. *Okay, keep going, give me everything you've got.*

'I have to live with you,' he gasps. 'I have to look at you every day, seeing her face looking back at me, knowing what she did to my brother! And I try,' he takes a step back as if contemplating cooling this off. 'Goddamn it, you little shit, I try every day not to lose it with you… I try to do what's right, JJ! I try to do what James would've wanted!'

'You treat me like *shit*,' I tell him, because why not? Why not now? He tries to do what my dad would have wanted? Bullshit! I step towards him. 'Is that what he wanted? For you to blame me for what my mother did? For

126

you to treat me like *I'm* the one who killed him? Like *I'm* the one who's crazy? Most days you can't even look me in the eye, and I didn't do anything wrong!'

I don't know why but it all floods out of me then. It's horrible, and I can't control it and I'm terrified of where this will lead me, but at the same time it's glorious, like ripping off a manky old plaster. I'm exploding from the inside and it feels so, so good.

'I didn't kill him!' I shout at Uncle Henry, pointing to my own chest. '*I* didn't kill anyone! But you punish me every single day! It wasn't me, Uncle Henry!'

He sort of nods and shrugs and shakes his head all at once, and as he lowers his head, he steps back again, and for some reason that just fires me up even more. I come at him, something dark and delicious thundering through my bones.

'*I'm not her!*' I scream at him then. 'I'm not my mother! I'm not like her! You can't keep treating me like I'm about to explode!'

Uncle Henry holds up both hands. 'You better calm the hell down, JJ.'

But all I can think about is how he has treated me: the times he's told me to get out of the house and stay out; the times he made me clean it from top to bottom; all the times he bitched at me and made me feel like a piece of shit on his shoe. And all the times I walked around his farm like a ghost, like a nothing, like nobody, with nobody to talk to, nobody to help me, nobody!

I shove him in the chest and my hands tighten with power, black smoke billowing now, spreading down my arms and out in the air around Henry. He looks shocked and worried and maybe even a little bit guilty.

'*You hate me!*' I hear myself scream, and it doesn't sound like me, it sounds like a lost little kid just wailing in pain. I shove him again and this time the power really kicks in. My hands feel like blocks of ice and the push sends him reeling towards the wall, where his head cracks against a framed picture I drew when I was little. The glass smashes and Uncle Henry stumbles, rubbing at his head and going down on one knee, his expression stunned.

Something in my head purrs *finish him, finish him, finish him...*

And the terrible thing is I know I could. I could finish anyone.

Uncle Henry holds up a hand. 'JJ?'

I race out of the room and don't look back.

22: Darcie

Ugh, it's no use. I slam down the lid of my laptop and sink further into the chair at my desk. I was stupid to think researching that goddamn mist would distract me from thinking about whatever the hell I saw last night. *Who the hell was my dad talking to? And why was he back so late?* Mom hasn't mentioned anything about it, but I imagine he'd blamed his disappearing act on work. She would accept that as gospel and doesn't like to pry where Bio-Chem is concerned. I guess that's another thing that makes us different.

I swivel back and forth for a moment, chewing my lip. My phone vibrates on the bed and I practically dive for it, swiping open the screen. *One new message.* My heart sinks; it's just some random junk mail. I toss my phone back on the bed and bury my face into the pillows. I text JJ three times this morning asking him what time my dad dropped him off, or if anything weird happened on the drive - no reply. *I swear, next time I see him I'm going to shove that phone right up his-*

'Are you awake, Miss Darcie?'

'Just a minute, Julia.' I roll my eyes as I unglue myself from the bed and open the door for her. Poor Julia, she's only small and the basket she's carrying is about three times the size of her.

'Any laundry today?'

I shake my head. 'I told you, I don't mind doing it myself…'

She laughs, 'Don't be silly, dear.' I pass her a pile of clothes from the hamper near my bed with a grin. That ought to keep her happy for a while. As she begins to shuffle towards the stairs, I call out for her.

'Julia, did you see my dad this morning?' The words leave my mouth before I really know why I'm asking.

'No, he left early today. I think he may have headed up to London.'

'Oh... I don't suppose you have the key to his office at all?' She looks me up and down as if she doesn't like where this is going. 'He borrowed one of my hard drives last week and I kinda need it.' She hesitates for a moment then reaches into her pocket and places a small silver key on the bedside table; her eyes never leaving mine. I practically salivate when I see it. That key could hold all the answers I need.

'Lock it when you're done and bring me back the key. If your mother catches you, I had nothing to do with it.' She raises her eyebrows and shuffles backwards out of the room, closing the door behind her. I wait until she is way out of earshot before grabbing the key and making my way down to Dad's office, hesitating outside the door for a moment, key poised in the lock.

I twist the handle and step inside. It hasn't changed in here since the last time I saw it. The walls are lined with large metal filing cabinets and in the centre a computer sits on an ornate desk. It is littered with paperwork and post-its. There's a noise from downstairs and I know I have to act fast. Darting towards the desk I rifle through anything I can get my hands on. Nothing. There's nothing here at all... Just a load of pointless emails and science journals. I try tugging open the drawers, but they are locked up like Fort Knox. I run my fingers through my hair and resist the urge to scream.

Have I lost my mind? I mean seriously, what the fuck am I doing here? What do I expect to find? I'm just about to leave when my hand brushes against the mouse and the monitor springs to life. I can't believe my luck—he's left it logged in! I lean into the screen and begin clicking through everything I can - emails, search history, files - then I see it... A zip folder tucked away in the corner of the desktop... '*CARSON Docs*'. My heart thumps. I feel sick. I click on the file and inside there are several more folders, all password protected apart from one. It's labelled '*JC*' and inside there is a copy of JJ's school report, medical records and something that looks like some sort of invoice. The noise from downstairs is getting closer and my hands begin to shake. I reach out to turn off the monitor and in typical Darcie fashion send a mass of files and papers whooshing onto the floor. *Shit.* I scramble to pick them up as I hear footsteps creaking up the stairs... *closer... closer...* I throw the items back on the desk and hope that my dad is far too tired to notice anything has moved before I rush for the door. As I yank it open, I come face-to-face with Jeremy.

'Whoa! What the hell?' I ask. He looks just as startled as I am, then peers over my shoulder to the desk. I follow his gaze before stepping out into the hallway and pulling the door closed. 'I was just looking for something.'

'Looking for what?'

'A hard drive.'

'A hard drive... really?'

'Yeah, what's it to you?' I push past him and head towards the stairs to my room. My body is still reeling from running into him like that, and from what I'd found on my dad's computer. Then I realise something. Pausing on the first step, I turn to face him with my arms folded. 'Wait. What were you going in there for?'

'I was just... Dad got back real late last night.'

'You noticed that too?' My stance softens and I peer down the staircase to check Julia and my mother are way out of earshot.

'Yeah, he was on his phone last night when your friend was here. He was talking to someone.'

'That's generally what phones are for, Jer.' I laugh but his face remains deadpan.

'It was a woman.' He glances up at the row of family photographs along the wall. 'I was worried that… It doesn't matter.' With that he storms off down the hall and into his room, slamming the door behind him.

A woman? I wonder as I peer up at the photographs and it all clicks into place. *Does my brother really think our dad is cheating?* There's just no way. Sure, our parents are fifty shades of fucked up, but I just can't see it. Not after all these years. Not after all they've been through together. Not after Jenna. I return to the safety of my room and pace back and forth. My head is so full of questions that I swear it's about to explode. Before I know what's come over me, I'm sitting on the bed surrounded by empty wrappers. I look down at my hands and I'm disgusted with myself. The shame I feel is so powerful that for a moment I just want to sink into the mattress and disappear. The girl in the mirror watches, smirking, and in my head, I hear her taunting me… '*Why wouldn't your father want to start a new family? You're pathetic!*' … '*Of course JJ doesn't want to text you back. You're disgusting.*' And the loudest of all - '*You will NEVER be perfect. You will NEVER be Jenna.*'

I run into the en suite and I bring it all up, all the words, all the hurt. But it's not enough. It will never be enough. I can feel the fire in my throat, the stinging in my eyes. I cry into the toilet bowl. It comes on in waves and I'm not really sure where from. I guess everything has just suddenly got too much for me. Everything that happened to Aunt Jenna, to Jared, the confrontation with Vicky, my mother, JJ. I feel it all coming to a head inside of me, a raging storm that I can no longer keep inside, but it feels so bittersweet to let it out. I grab the edges of the bowl and hoist myself up, wiping an arm across my face.

I stumble towards the sink for water, for a towel, for anything that will get rid of the evidence of what I have just done, get rid of the awful sour taste. Only, when I reach the sink there she is, the girl, staring at me in the bathroom mirror, cool and collected. I cry and I keep crying. I go to take a step but suddenly I find my body giving way. I fall to the ground and my head collides against the edge of the sink. *Crack!*

Is this it? Is this how it goes down? I lay on the floor, unable to move, just staring into the pattern on the tiles. The pain in my head is unbearable and my body feels so weak. My last thought is a funny one. I think about the irony of how the same thing happened to Jared and how I'd kept it secret for JJ's sake. After all, he was only trying to save me. *But where is he now? Where is he when I need him more than ever before?*

'JJ…'

My eyes begin to close, and the world goes black.

23: JJ

Somehow, I find myself back at the cottage.

I have nothing on me - no phone, no money, no notebook, nothing. It's just me in my jeans and t-shirt, biting my nails in fear as I approach my mother's childhood home. I'm trembling, with what I don't know. Fear, anger, regret, love, all of them. I'm sort of crying too, like some pussy baby, like the weirdo kid, the oddball Uncle Henry says I am, the freak they all think I am. I'm starting to feel defeated. I'm starting to feel like there is no point denying what I am. No point fighting back.

This makes me cry and I don't care. I'm sobbing and snorting as I weave my way through the overgrown garden, this time alone, this time without Darcie. For a moment I see her face in my head, as our foreheads touched and our eyes met and… we nearly kissed, or at least it felt like it at the time but now my dark mind convinces me this is ludicrous. Why the hell would a girl like that even think about kissing a boy like me? She's just nice, that's all, just kind, like her dad said. Just taking pity on me, that's what it is.

The dark thoughts increase as I creep around to the back of the cottage and let myself in. They sneak up on me at first, sly and malicious.

As if she was going to kiss you! What a joke.

I steal into the dark shadows of the old cottage and inhale the stench of mildew and thick dust, and something else lingering just underneath, like secrets and guilt.

She pities you, that's what it is.

I tighten my fists and wonder what the hell I am doing here. I stand by the grease smeared window for a few moments just breathing it all in. I am trying to find him again, the hangman, the spirit, whatever it was Darcie saw behind me. Maybe I can feel him... I don't know. I can feel something.

Or is it just the mist? I look down at my cold hands and sure enough it's there, wisps of grey easing out from between my clenched fingers. I swallow the dry lump in my throat and gaze around at the kitchen my mother used to eat her breakfast in as a small girl.

You're a joke, a freak, a weirdo... You're nothing and they are all right about you!

Well, maybe they are. And maybe that's okay.

I lift my fists and stare at the mist. It thickens and darkens as if it is pleased I am paying it attention. I feel my fists tingling within it, power emanating from it and seeping into me. How is this possible? And then I think of my mother and my grandmother and who else before her? Did they have this too? This curse or this gift? I'm sure my mother saw it as a curse. They tried to warn me, tried to tell me to stay happy, to find things to smile about. Does that mean something failed the day Mum killed my dad?

I suddenly need to know. What happened that day? What changed in her? What snapped? I spin suddenly and place my hands against the thin glass of the kitchen window. It implodes in a shower of glass before I even touch it. It felt me coming. I gasp and jump back but I want more. I turn on my heel and grab the closest thing to me, an old wooden stool I remember my mother hoisting me up onto when I skinned my knee in the garden one day.

From the stool I could see out the kitchen window, see the ducks and the hens wandering happily around the garden and my grandmother hanging washing out on the line. They had always seemed so happy, so carefree, so sweet and kind. Was it all an act? A lie? Were they laughing at me too? Pretending to love and nurture me so that one day it would be even worse when it all came crashing down? Did my mother always know this would happen to her and to me?

I need to talk to her. I need to see her but Uncle Henry is not going to let that happen. I touch the stool, place my hands around the seat and the whole thing collapses under my touch. My mouth falls open as I stare at the crumbled mess of wood at my feet. There must be answers here somewhere!

I run from the room and start ransacking the place. Yanking open cupboards, flinging back rugs, checking for loose floorboards, ripping pictures from the wall.

You are one unhinged crazy little freak…You're dangerous too, just like her. You need locking up.

The mist is black now and I can feel it is as angry and lost as me. As I search the cottage from top to bottom, it is with me, it is my friend and my ally and I know it won't turn on me like last time. Maybe that was because Darcie was here and it wanted her to go. Now it helps me; it trashes the house with me. Everything smashes and crumbles as I touch it. I look in the bathroom and I only get a glimpse of my deranged face in the old, cracked mirror before it explodes everywhere with a violent crash, splinters of glass spraying the air.

I duck back out and run downstairs. I have nothing. This was pointless!

I'm crossing the lounge, heading for the kitchen in a hurry when I see a face at the window. My eyes widen, my mouth falls open, my breath hitches in my throat. One second they are there and the next they are gone. I charge through to the kitchen, everything I touch and bump into splintering into pieces.

'Hey!' I yell out. 'Hey you!'

I shove open the crumbling back door and it flies from its hinges like it's been detonated or something. I stop, breathing hard and fast and staring around but I can't see anything at all. There is no one there. But there was! And it wasn't a dark figure or a ghostly entity either…

I plough through the garden and run around to the front, just in time to catch a figure dressed all in black racing out of sight.

'Hey!' I yell again and give chase.

I charge after them, picking up pace, running as fast as I can down the overgrown paths but I can't see them, not ahead, not anywhere. I slow down, out of breath and choked up inside. I gaze down at my hands to see that the mist has deserted me. There are a few open cuts on my palms though, one bleeding quite badly. I hadn't even felt it, but now it's starting to sting a little. I guess the exploding bathroom mirror gave me something to remember it by.

I'm pondering this and the figure in black and thinking the best thing I could do right now is find Darcie, talk to Darcie, because she is so calm, so cool, so everything I am not. God, I need her, I want her, and we nearly kissed, how is that possible? How could that have happened to *me*? I'm running this all through my fucked up little mind when I feel the arms wrap around me from behind, and for a small moment I'm strangely relieved, because I think, it must be the hangman! The ghost! Whatever the hell this is that cursed my mother and her mother and made them all go crazy! He wants me too and he can have me…

But then I hear the familiar giggles and I smell their warm beery breath and Andrew Hart steps in front of me while Frankie Simpson tightens his hold on me and they both look very, very happy to see me.

'Wanna know how Jared is?' Andrew asks before throwing a punch into my mid-section. I don't think either of them are interested in my thoughts or my replies, as the punch is followed by Frankie yanking my head back with a hand entwined in my hair.

'He's a cabbage because of you!' he snarls into my ear before shoving me down on my knees.

'I didn't touch him,' I gasp and stare at my hands, wanting the mist, needing the mist and it's there, it's coming, faint grey puffs easing out from my palms.

Frankie kicks me in the back and I go sprawling into the dust face first, my glasses skittering to one side.

'Yeah right, you were there that night, we know you were!'

Andrew leaps forward and fires a right hook up under my chin. I'm thrown backwards, this time landing on my arse as the power of the punch ricochets through my skull.

'You got a lot to answer for you little psycho freak!' he yells.

Frankie is leering over me, grinning maniacally as he lifts a foot, preparing to bring it down on my ribs. I roll away and as I do I lift my hands. They don't see the mist - no one does but Darcie and why is that? Why her?

But I don't have time to wonder. The power of it repels Frankie, throwing him off balance and sending him crashing back into someone's garden fence. He goes down with the panels and it's just me and Andrew. I wait until he's coming at me with his fists before I push out with mine.

I make contact; I don't need to but I don't want him to know what's happening, and the force of the mist sends him sprawling backwards, his arms and legs pinwheeling for balance and losing the fight. He lands in the river and I sit up, gasping.

'JJ!' someone yells at me in a hissed voice.

I look up and see a car I recognise parked at the end of the walk. Darcie's dad is behind the wheel and beckoning to me urgently.

'JJ, get in!'

I snatch my glasses, get up quickly, and glance around once to see Frankie scrambling about in someone's garden and Andrew splashing through the water to come at me again. I don't have any choice so I take off and sprint towards the waiting car.

24: Darcie

'Okay, open them.'

I feel her cool hands leave my face, Aunt Jenna, and I am standing in my room in front of the mirror wearing one of her dresses. It's an aquamarine number that flows out from the waist down, the bodice dotted with shimmering gems. I'm blown away. I look so new… so different… so *beautiful*. It's like it's not even real, not even me. Jenna's standing behind me, grinning from ear to ear and trying not to cry. There's a tap on the door and I hear voices. I watch in the reflection as she flashes a knowing smile and leaves. In her place, JJ enters. He looks so handsome in his oversized suit and I suppress a chuckle as he makes his way towards me with a bow.

'Are you sure you want to do this?' I ask. 'School dances aren't exactly your scene.'

'But you are.'

I blush and turn away. He walks over to the bed and takes a seat. I watch him in the mirror and pretend to be adjusting my hair as he clocks me staring. My stomach is all in knots, like a thousand butterflies are flying around inside of it, desperate to break free. Rubbing my hands, I let out a breath and join him on the bed.

'Do you want to know a secret?' He places a hand on my knee and the electricity is undeniable. He doesn't wait for me to respond. 'Not so long ago we sat here, like this.'

'I remember.'

'I can't forget it.' Our eyes meet. 'But, do you know what I regret the most?'

'What?' My heart is pounding, I can feel it throbbing in my throat.

'Not doing this.' He leans in and our lips connect; it feels like magic. I don't want to pull away from it. I don't want it to stop. There's a symphony in the air all around us that only I can hear, and the dust motes dance across it. I lay back on the bed, taking the weight of him on top of me. We kiss, and we kiss, and we - He cries out.

'What's wrong? Did I do something?' A black mist wraps around him, growing from his fingertips like vines. His eyes grow dark. He looks away ashamed, but I reach out for him, assuring him that it's okay and that I'm not afraid. I accept him just the way he is, all the dark parts and all the light. He grins back at me, only he is no longer JJ Carson, the boy from the river... He is shifting, changing, becoming something else. Something evil. Something wrong. Something now wearing the face of Jared Wheeler. It presses its thumbs into my neck, and I can't breathe. The pressure is too much. I try to call out, to apologise for what we did, but I can't. I'm choking. Fading out. I look across at the girl in the mirror but she's not there. Even she has given up on me. They all have. The voices in the hallway are no longer audible. Even the voices in my head have grown silent. *So, this is it? This is what it comes to? Just me, Jared, and the end.*

*

My eyes open.

There are voices in the hallway. A tap on the door. I look down and I'm wrapped in a green-blue blanket. There's something cold stuck to my arm and it itches. I hear breathing. People talking. It's Julia, and my mother. They're talking about me like I'm not even here. My throat feels dry and scratchy and my eyes sting as they adjust to the bright artificial light.

'Okay, thank you doctor.' There is a flicker of something different in my mother's voice. Something vulnerable. *Worry?* I groan and I pull myself up on the pillows.

'Miss Darcie!' Julia's hand grips mine. 'Oh, thank heavens.'

'Julia, how-'

'Don't strain too hard, darling.' My mother rushes over to my side and her face is alight with relief. Then, catching me smile back, her face hardens. 'We can't have you causing more of a scene, can we?'

Julia laughs then notes how deadpan she is and stops.

'Mom, what happened?'

'You tell me. Doctor Fisher ran some tests. You've been in and out for a while. Can you believe she even had the audacity to interrogate me about how I choose to parent?' She laughs. 'Thinks I'm not feeding you enough. So, I said to her, look, I don't know what you feed your kids, but Malcolm and I only buy the finest, organic-'

'Mom...'

'What is it, dear?' I glance at Julia for support, but she suddenly finds something on the floor far more interesting than me.

'I have something...' I begin, but the sound of a phone ringing ricochets off every surface. My mother rummages through her purse and sighs before placing it to her ear. 'Alyssa Duffield. Oh, hi Pam. Yes, yes, I did. I know. I couldn't believe it either-'

'Mom.'

'Oh, sorry dear.' She clasps a hand over the phone, and I can just make out the rapid mumbles of her friend coming down the line. 'You need your rest. Julia, my coat. Sweetheart, we need to go get Jeremy, but we'll be back to collect you as soon as Doctor Fisher says you can leave.' She nods for Julia to join her and the pair bustle out of the room, leaving me in the overwhelming quiet.

As soon as they are gone, I try to relax. Try to remember how it was I got here. I was in my bedroom, Julia came in... *Ugh. Why the fuck is everything such a blur!?* Then I see it, creeping up from the bottom of the bed, those black, burnt hands. Thick mist. The face of Jared Wheeler. I scream out and cover my eyes and wait for pain. But it doesn't come. I open my eyes and the creature has gone. Disappeared like a puff of... well, smoke.

It can't have been real. None of it can. Zombie Jared. The hangman. It's got to be this sickening guilt toying with my mind. I sit up and the room spins a little, I wait for it to settle before placing my feet on the ground and wobble towards the door. I open it a crack, check the coast is clear, and then make my way down the hall. My face feels warm and I know that it must be pretty banged up because my eye hurts when I place a hand against it. It feels rough too, like there's dried blood caked on my forehead.

When I reach the front desk, I ring the bell and wait but nobody comes. I consider trying the computer, but the sound of the automatic doors causes me to jump back and a smartly dressed couple pass by me accompanied by a doctor. I duck into the shadows.

'Thank you, Mr and Mrs Wheeler. Of course, I'll call you if there's any change.' *Wheeler?* I wait until they leave and follow the doctor back along the corridor. He looks back at me a few times, but I slip in and out of view. Suddenly, I lose him by the row of elevators, but not before he drops off his clipboard at the nurse's station. I know I have to act fast, and hover by the hand sanitiser as my eyes scan down the list of names and ward allocations. I finally find it, the room that Jared's in. *I have to see him. I have to know that he can't hurt me any longer… that he can't tell anyone what we did to him.*

I snake through the corridors and along the row of endless doors. When I finally reach the room, the dread hits me like a freight train. Who knows what I'll find? Do I really want to see Jared lying there, his brain scrambled like eggs? I know he's an asshole and that he deserves everything he got and more, but…

I step inside. The room is eerily still but for the soft *beep, beep, beep* of the blood pressure monitor, and the whirring of the ventilator. He's there, in the bed, strapped up with tubes and wires. *Wow, JJ, what the fuck did we do?* I approach. Shaking. I stand there by the edge of the bed for the longest time, just staring at him. Then I see him in my mind's eye. See his hands brushing against me. Feel his breath on my neck. I'm angry. Hurt. Disgusted. I lean against his ear and whisper, part of me hoping that he's somewhere inside there, still able to hear me.

'How's it feel to be trapped? People talking about you like you're not even here. Touching you.' I grab the ventilation tube and roll it around in my fingers. 'You're fucking done. You can't hurt me anymore. You can't hurt anyone… and I'm glad.' I squeeze the tube for a second as tears roll down my cheeks. Something in the forefront of my mind is enjoying this, it's telling me to squeeze the tube tighter. It's laughing as his body rocks and vibrates as it desperately hungers for oxygen. *What am I doing? This isn't right… This isn't me!* I look up and notice the girl in the mirror across the room grinning from ear to ear. I jump back, releasing my grip on the tube and run my fingers through my hair. When I look back at the mirror, all I see is me. Sweat dripping from my bruised brow, I move towards Jared and lean into him once more.

'I'm sorry.'

I turn to leave but his hand clamps down on my wrist. I look back at him in horror, but his face is completely still, eyes closed as if he's just sleeping. I peel his fingers from my arm and head for the door. I'm almost out when two voices from outside cause me to stop dead in my tracks. *Shit!* I look around for somewhere to hide but come up empty. The only options are the little bathroom in the corner or getting down on my knees and crawling under the bed, but it's far too risky. I am frozen solid. My heart pounding in my ears. I watch, wide-eyed, as the handle moves down. Then it stops. I hear laughter then the sound of footsteps moving off down the hall, towards the vending machines at the end.

I dart out of the room and pull the door closed behind me. I can't believe how close that was. What would I have told them if I was caught? How could I explain my way out of this one? I'm shaking like a leaf as I walk away from the room, down the corridor, around the corner and right into Vicky Marshall. She spills her hot chocolate against her chest with a gasp, looks up at me aghast, then off in the direction I had come. She knows exactly where I've been. I can see it in her eyes.

'Wow. You're absolutely relentless, aren't you?' She frowns, throwing the cup into the bin next to her and walking right up to me until we are almost touching. I swallow hard.

25: JJ

Mr Duffield drives us back into Fortune's Well. 'I think that might need stitches, you know,' he says with a furrowed brow, nodding at my hand.

I'm sitting in the passenger seat, straightening out my glasses and getting blood all over them in the process. He reaches for the glove compartment and yanks it open to reveal a box of tissues.

'Help yourself. It looks deep.'

I tug out a wad and press them into my hand, folding my fingers down over them. I breathe in deeply and out slowly. I am suddenly bone tired and I know if I risked even resting my head back on the seat I would be out in seconds.

'It's your nose too,' says Mr Duffield, gesturing at my face.

Christ. I pull out another bunch of tissues and mop up my nose. 'Thanks,' I mumble, because I don't know what the hell else to say. 'Good timing,' I add, by way of making conversation and avoiding me nodding off.

'I'd say so,' he grins widely. 'Those guys were kicking your ass - do you know them? I kinda thought they looked familiar.'

'Jared Wheeler's friends,' I shrug at him. 'They don't like me much.'

Mr Duffield nods in sympathy. 'Well anyway, looked like you were giving as good as you got. I saw one of them go flying through that fence!' He glances at me with wide eyes and an approving nod. 'That was awesome, by the way. What was that? Karate or something?'

I snort a laugh. 'No. Nothing like that. I dunno, I guess my uncle's been teaching me to box, for self-defence, you know. It comes in handy.'

'That's good of him,' he nods.

'You can just drop me off at the farm if you like, Mr Duffield.'

He shakes his head at me. 'Oh no, I'm taking you to the hospital, JJ. That cut needs looking at.'

'Oh no, really, it's fine. I don't want to make a fuss,' I try arguing. 'And besides, my uncle is really good with cuts and stuff, he'll fix it up for me.'

'I insist! No arguments.' Mr Duffield raises his eyebrows at me and I get a brief glimpse of what it must be like having him for a father. I really don't want to be in his car or go to the hospital but I find myself falling silent and giving in.

'How are things with your uncle?' he's asking me next. 'Do you get on well?'

He's a nosy kind of guy, I guess, but maybe it's because of Darcie. My paranoia creeps stealthily back to accompany me to the hospital. Yeah, of course, what kind of father would be okay with their precious daughter hanging around with the town freak? He's only being nice to me to suss me out so that he can warn her off or forbid her from seeing me.

My body feels so exhausted it's like a bag of jelly just lolling and sloshing in the seat as the car rolls along. Mr Duffield seems to be picking up speed and as the car rolls up and over a speed bump, my head rocks back and makes contact with the head rest. And that's it. My eyes are drooping, my eyelids so heavy I can barely keep them apart.

'You tired?'

'Ummm…'

'JJ? Did you hit your head back there?'

'No, no nothing like that...' I rub at my face violently with both hands. The movement sets the cut off again and fresh blood seeps through the tissues. 'Oh, crap.'

'Right that's it, definitely no arguments,' says Mr Duffield. 'We are going to check you out young man. You're looking pretty drowsy to me.'

I try to talk. But I can't. And what would I say anyway? It's not the cut, I didn't hit my head, it's not the fight... I know what it is. It's the mist. It's been with me all day, since I shoved Uncle Henry this morning and trashed the cottage after that. Oh God, what did I do? Uncle Henry will never forgive me. He'll never look at me or speak to me again. I proved him right, that's what I did! All of a sudden, I could just cry. I don't want to be like this! I don't want to be this person!

A tear escapes my eye as I turn my groggy head to face him. 'Mr Duffield, could you do me a favour? If possible?...Please?'

'Sure JJ, just ask. Ask away.'

My eyes close again and I force them open and lean over my knees. 'You know what my mum did, right? You know how my dad died?'

'Yes JJ, I'm so sorry. Everybody knows,' he replies softly. 'Do you want to talk about it? My kids tell me I'm a really good listener.'

I breathe in and out again. 'My uncle worries about me,' I try to explain and even as I speak, I can hear my voice getting thicker as the sleep tries to claim me. 'He thinks I'm gonna end up the same as her, you know. So he won't let me see her. He's not letting me see her anymore Mr Duffield.'

Mr Duffield looks at me with a stern frown. 'I see.'

'And I need to see her,' I go on, my eyes closed now, my head bumping against the window. 'I really, really need to see her... I need answers...'

'I can help you.'

I smile against the cold glass.

'We're at the hospital, JJ, you with me?'

The car stops and the engine dies and I feel him leaning over me. His hand brushes against my forehead before he checks my pulse.

'It's okay,' he says and I hear his door open and the car rocks as he climbs out. He opens my side gently and I nearly fall out but he catches me and smooths my hair away from my face. I'm going down so fast I can barely open my mouth let alone walk. I have seconds left to try to talk, to thank him, to ask for Darcie, but every time I try to move my mouth the solid exhaustion seizes me and I just can't.

'It's okay, JJ,' Mr Duffield is saying. 'I've got you. We'll get you checked out, okay? You're gonna be just fine and you can trust me, okay? I'm gonna help you, JJ. I'm gonna help you with everything.'

I just about manage a smile of thanks before the black consumes me.

26: Darcie

I'm fearing the worst as her eyes give me a once over and every part of me tenses. Seriously, this is the last thing I need—Vicky Marshall swooping in to tell me how awful I am. I already know what people think of me. I already know what they see. I see it too. The strangest thing happens though, her face seems to soften. I look into it and I don't see the bitchy, popular girl who makes it through life by climbing over, *and under*, everybody else. Instead, I see something real, something human. I see the friend I made when I first moved to the town of Fortune's Well. The girl who reached out and made me feel a little less alone.

'What the hell happened?'

For a moment I think she's talking about our friendship, to which I don't have a solid answer. Then I notice her eyes lingering on my forehead.

'It's nothing, I just fell…'

She looks me up and down and then takes my arm. 'When I saw you here, I thought you were after Jared again.'

I laugh, although inside I know she isn't joking. There's a silence between us, it's calming yet uncomfortable. I shrug out of her grasp.

'Your shirt, shit, sorry.'

'It's fine. Plus, it tasted like crap anyway.'

I think about asking her if she's burnt but I know the truth. Vicky has been padding out her bra since the age of twelve, not that she still needs to. There's no way it has soaked through to her skin.

'Let's get you washed up.'

'Me?' She laughs. 'Have you seen the state of you, babe?' I frown as she slips her arm around mine and together, we make our way into the toilets.

'We're a right pair, aren't we?' She grabs a wad of paper towels from the dispenser on the wall and begins blotting at her chest, then carries on rambling about Frankie and Andrew and a few of the other girls from our year, but I'm not listening. My eyes are firmly fixed on the edges of the sink. Something is scurrying around in my mind, a memory I'm so desperate to get a hold of.

Crack.

I see Jared Wheeler's face slam against the side of the ceramic and my body jolts. I place my hand on the cool surface and dig my fingers into it.

Crack.

This time I see myself falling, colliding with the side, and I feel the awful crunch of bone. I touch the dried blood above my eye and wince. It's tender. Raw. I look up at my reflection, mouth agape, as I remember exactly what happened to me. Exactly how I had purged and purged, but it just wasn't enough. How the girl in the mirror had stood there and smirked. How the world began to spin, and I fell. But there was something else, something important that I was missing. I try so hard to clamp down on the memory that it makes my head ache and I wobble once again.

'Whoa, you okay, babe?' She asks, quickly rushing to my side and holding me upright. She scans my body up and down and I feel her hand on my lower back release slightly as if she is scared to apply too much pressure. I wonder if she knows my secret, the one only I know. If she didn't already, she must have some idea now. Her lips move and I think this is it, this is where she confronts me. Tells me what I am doing is stupid. It's wrong. The logical part of me knows that it is, but somehow, I just can't seem to stop. The words are bubbling away inside of her, threatening to spill out over those lips and flood the silence.

'So, you're here to see Jared?' I step back.

'Yeah, Frankie and Andrew were here earlier, too. We had to wait for his parents to leave though. Only allowed a certain number of people at once.' She takes my place in front of the sink and checks her make-up in the mirror.

'Is there any news about what happened to him? He was talking last time we spoke about him, I guess he got worse?'

'He was slipping in and out at first. Mostly talking shit.' She smears on her peach lip-gloss and smacks her lips together. 'Guess some things never change.'

'Must be hard, him being in that condition... Not just for you but him too. Stuck inside his own head like that. Able to hear everyone coming and going, but not able to do anything about it.'

'Wow. Morbid much?' She laughs. 'At least he's keeping his hands where I can see 'em.' I notice the way she scans me up and down in the mirror. I think about the burnt, black hands crawling up the end of my hospital bed, and the way Jared had latched onto me as I went to leave his room, and I shudder.

'Vicky... Jared and I... Nothing-'

'Oh, I know.'

I'm baffled, just staring at her wide-eyed. If she knew nothing was going on, why was she so hard on me?

'Let's just say you're not the only one he's got a little touchy with.'

I go to ask her more, but something about her expression tells me not to pry.

'Then, why? Why be such a bitch to me the other day?'

'I was jealous, I guess... I mean, look at you! *Miss Darcie Duffield.* Long legs. Blonde Hair. Dad who's loaded.

A real Miss America. It's not exactly like I'm Cinderella is it?' She leans up against the wall arms folded. 'Face it, DeeDee. You're hot. Pretty sure half the school thinks so. And not just the boys.'

I don't know what to say. There's no way so many people think that about me, and even if I am pretty on the outside, heaven knows I am fucked up on the inside. Ugly. Broken. Then I notice Vicky's face, her eyes look so full of hurt. *Shit.* Damn, Darcie, you've been so caught up in your own mind you've neglected to ask your friends how they're doing… After all, if I can put on a mask every day, who's to say that they can't too? Who's to say that Frankie Simpson isn't super sensitive, Ben Evans isn't heartbroken, or that Vicky Marshall isn't incredibly insecure…

'You're beautiful, Vick. Really. You are.'

I walk over and wrap an arm around her, pulling her into a hug. There's another quiet moment between us, only this time I can take it. She pulls away and checks her make-up once again.

'Okay, enough of this soppy crap.' She wipes at her mascara. 'You're *totally* gay for me.'

'*Totally.*' I laugh. 'C'mon. Let's go grab a drink. I hear the hot chocolate here's delicious.'

*

Wow… She really wasn't kidding.

I toss the empty cup into the bin and roll my tongue along my teeth. It was nice to spend time with Vicky and just act like girls again. I guess I'd kinda missed that. But for now, there is a bitter taste forming in my mouth, and it isn't just from the hot chocolate. To my horror, Julia and my mother are nowhere to be found and Doctor Fisher is not allowing me to leave without parental consent. *Seriously? Sure, I fell but I'm okay now... Aren't I?* I start to recall all the strange visions and things that have been happening to me since I arrived here and find myself unable to answer the question.

Doctor Fisher had some questions for me too. She started asking me about my parents, about my brother, she even gave me this stupid flyer about free counselling sessions. As if anyone on this earth is qualified enough to figure *me* out.

That's it, I can't take this. The silence. Vicky has gone off to find Andrew and Frankie, and I can't sit here any longer. I need to get out. I make my way out into the hall, a girl on a mission, and march right up to the front desk. But a voice around the corner causes me to stop in my tracks. *Dad? What the hell is he doing here?* Then I see the familiar mop of blonde hair beside him, JJ Carson, the boy from the river, the boy from my room. My heart thumps. He looks hurt. My dad dabs at his face with some tissue as a nurse rushes over to them, asking what happened.

Dad turns to face my way, but I duck back into the shadows. I want to approach, I want to find out what he's doing here, and if JJ is okay. But something in my brain is telling me to keep my distance, at least for now. My eyes pass over JJ's face and then to my father's piercing eyes and I begin shaking uncontrollably. In my head the fragments of my memory begin to glue together. I remember it all. The computer. The files. *What the hell is going on here? Why all the secrets? The fight with Jenna. The late-night phone call.* I lean up against the wall and watch the boy I just met, and the man who raised me, and feel sick to my stomach as I realise which one of them I know the least about.

154

27: JJ

I wince and bite down on my lower lip as the nurse applies the paper stitches to my hand. Mr Duffield is standing on my other side and I'm perched on the edge of a hospital bed holding another bunch of tissues to my nose.

'Did you hit your nose too?' the nurse glances at me and asks. She reminds me of my PE teacher at school. Curly black hair scraped into a high bun, an athletic physique, and a no-nonsense expression.

'No,' I tell her, just wanting to get the hell out of there. 'It's just a nosebleed, I think. I had one the other day.'

'You should get it looked at, if it's a new thing,' she says, giving me a look that makes me feel about six years old. 'Make an appointment with your GP, okay?'

'I agree,' says Mr Duffield, nodding at me when I look up at him. 'And I told you it needed stitches.'

I just shrug and gaze at the wall while the nurse finishes with my hand. I don't want to be here, being fussed over. I still feel bone tired, like just holding my head up is an unreasonably monumental effort.

'You should get checked out,' Mr Duffield says again. 'You passed out in my car you know. I just about managed to walk you in here. Do you remember anything?'

I shrug again. 'Think I was just tired...'

'You think you fell *asleep*?' the nurse questions in a tone that suggests how ridiculous she thinks that is.

I nod uneasily as they both glare at me. 'I think so, yeah, I was just super tired... I didn't sleep last night.'

Mr Duffield and the nurse swap a look that I am unable to read. It's stern and yet worried and my stomach is a horrible mess and I just want to get the hell out of here.

I've got so much explaining to do at home, it's just a joke, and that's before I even start thinking about the mist and the cottage and my mother… God, I just want to close my eyes.

Perhaps sensing this, the nurse fluffs up the pillow on the bed and jerks her head towards it. 'Go on,' she says. 'Get some shut-eye. Your hand is fine but we'll keep you in for a few hours in case you did pass out. That okay with you?'

I just nod, pull up my legs and let my head hit that deliciously plumped up pillow. I feel them watching me as I curl up on my side and close my eyes.

'We need to call his parents or carers,' the nurse says to Mr Duffield. 'Do you happen to know their numbers?'

'Ah, it's complicated,' Mr Duffield says and then I hear footsteps as the two of them move away from the bed. There is some murmuring between them at the door and I hear the nurse saying:

'Uh huh, I see. I see.'

'Basically neglectful from what I can tell… But I'll go there now and pick him up okay? It won't take long.'

What? Did Mr Duffield call Uncle Henry neglectful or was he talking about someone else? I try to lift my head or roll over, but I just can't. I am swamped by a blanket of heavy exhaustion that I just don't want to fight anymore. I let them go. I let them all go and allow myself to drift away.

*

When I wake up, there is someone standing over me.

My heart leaps into my throat and some dark dredges of a shadowy dream drift away quickly as an instant fear seizes me. But then I see her face appearing above mine. Darcie.

Shit, I want to kiss her. I want to grab her perfect face with both of my hands and pull it down to mine and…

She's smiling but she looks confused and concerned. Her hands are over mine and I'm suddenly horribly conscious of the sheen of dribble I can feel on my chin. I push myself up on the bed and drag my damaged hand over my mouth.

'Darcie…'

'What the hell happened to you?' she says in a low, hissed voice. Her eyes flit nervously to the door which is slightly ajar.

I look her over and clock the swollen eye and cut to her forehead. 'Me? What the hell happened to you?'

She lifts a hand and touches the cut gingerly before wincing and smiling. 'God, nothing. I fainted or something at home. Ridiculous, I know. My mother totally overreacted and dragged me down here. *So* embarrassing. What about you?'

Now it's my turn to glance nervously at the door. 'Anyone out there?'

She turns swiftly, reaches out and clicks the door shut. She's back at my side and grabbing my hand in seconds. 'Your turn. What happened?'

I drop my head into my other hand. 'Shit. *Everything.*'

'Just take it one thing at a time then. Why did my dad bring you here?'

'He found me,' I try to explain. 'I got in a fight with Jared's friends and your dad pulled up and got me to jump in.' I try to read her face but it's strangely still and closed off as if a million thoughts are racing around inside jostling for attention. Her hand tightens on mine so I take that as a cue to go on. 'I had a fight with Uncle Henry,' I sigh. 'A bad one. Really bad, Darcie. He's probably packed my bags by now.'

She lifts her eyebrows, questioning me and now her expression is so anguished I can barely stand it. 'The mist?'

'Yeah,' I hang my head in shame. 'So, I ran off, ended up at the cottage.' Her eyes widen again and her hand squeezes even tighter. 'Nothing happened,' I try to assure her. 'I was fine. I lost my shit and smashed it up a bit though. But then I saw someone looking in at me.'

'What?' Darcie's head pulls back on her shoulders. 'Who was it?'

'I dunno,' I shrug. 'Not even sure if it was real, or you know…'

She nods, understanding. 'So, let me guess, you ran after them?'

'Yep, but they'd gone and I ran into Andrew and Frankie instead.'

'Oh God, JJ,' Darcie closes her eyes briefly. 'Please, please tell me you didn't use the mist on them?'

I grimace and stare down at my injured hand, turning it over to expose the paper stitches. I offer her a measly shrug as explanation. 'I didn't mean to, Darcie. It just happened.'

'That's the problem, right there,' she says, suddenly grabbing the seat of the plastic chair beside the bed and yanking it forward. She sits quickly and hunches up over me, still holding my other hand, which I take as a good sign. 'You can't control it, can you?' she asks me. 'Whether you mean to use it or not, subconsciously, or whatever, it comes out anyway, whenever you're in a fight or flight situation. Am I right?'

I nod miserably. 'Looks that way.'

'JJ,' she whispers, and for a moment her eyes seem shiny like she is battling tears. 'We have to figure this out. *Really* figure this out, I mean. We need to go somewhere quiet and safe and research this whole thing, the mist, the cottage, your mum, *everything*.'

'Okay,' I agree, my voice dropping lower as I hear footsteps coming towards the door. 'As soon as we're both out of here. I'll have to see where I stand with Uncle Henry and after that, I'll call you, okay?'

'Okay,' she says, then twists around as the door is pushed open and Mr Duffield reappears this time with someone in tow. 'Oh, hi,' Darcie straightens up and I can't see her face but she sounds happy.

Vicky Marshall strides in like she owns the place. Jesus, no. I mean, what the actual hell? Right away I can feel that cold tingling in my hands again. I pull away from Darcie and clench my fists and just glare at them all.

'So, you found each other then?' Mr Duffield says jovially, as the two of them shuffle into the room. 'Darcie, I heard what happened, are you all right, darling?'

She nods at him. 'Yeah, I'm fine, Dad, I swear. I've been looked at.'

He breathes out slowly in relief. 'Well, I'm sure your mother will be making a GP appointment just in case. I just got back from seeing JJ's uncle and bumped into Vicky here. She was looking for you, Darcie. And JJ?'

I tear my eyes away from Vicky's self-satisfied smirk to look at him. 'What?'

'Your uncle is a tad hungover I'm afraid and unable to drive,' Mr Duffield rolls his eyes and releases a small puff of a sigh. 'But he agreed I could drive you home as soon as we're finished here, is that all right?'

I glance back at Vicky, and she's eyeballing me, all right. Her eyes all narrowed and glinting with malice, her lips turned up in a nasty little smile, and as I stare, she raises her eyebrows at me, daring me, teasing me. God, I hate her. Why the hell is Darcie all friendly with her again? This makes no sense. My hands are cold and getting colder and when I glance down, there it is, my friend the mist. I look back at Vicky and grin at her.

28: Darcie

Something happened back there. He won't admit it, but it did. I think he forgets that I can see it too - the mist. I saw the way it swirled around his fists like a tornado. He caught me looking and it stopped him somehow, soothed him. But there was something there in his eyes when he looked at Vicky. A darkness. My stomach twists in knots when I think about it, and it feels as though a bowling ball is lodged in the back of my throat. *Is he starting to enjoy this? The strange power he has.*

'I'll text you tomorrow, I promise.' I lean in and hug Vicky, but she raises her eyebrows and smirks.

'As if! I'm coming with you.'

My ears prick up as JJ huffs behind me. I wait for him to say something, but he doesn't.

'Two words, DeeDee... *Henry "Hotty" Carson.'*

'Actually, that's thr-'

'I'm coming with you. Besides, I can't leave you alone with *him*. We still don't know what happened to Jared.'

Great. This is exactly what I need. How the heck am I supposed to talk to JJ with Vicky tagging along? One more whiff of suspicion and that's it, she'll have the entire town chasing him down with pitchforks.

My dad has gone to sign me out whilst the three of us wait underneath the huge blue and red sculpture in the courtyard. It's a strange design, a pyramid of pencils that all spin around one another. I've always wondered why it was here... What do pencils have to do with a hospital? I look over at JJ and smile as he peers up at the metal frame above. The first time I'd seen him he was sketching. What better way to end our trip to the hospital than here? I laugh aloud and Vicky clears her throat, the noise dragging me back to reality with a thump.

'Does *he* always follow you around now?'

'Does *she* really need to come with us?'

JJ's words make me cringe, I wait for Vicky's response.

'What are you even doing here?' she snaps.

'Ask your friends.'

'My friends? Really? You're the freak who-'

'Guys, can we not.' I stand between them, arms outstretched just in case things get any more heated. My eyes flick towards JJ's clenched fists for a second, relieved that they are mist free. I can't believe this; Vicky and I are finally clearing the air and now I am going to be forced to pick a side again.

'You don't know anything about me,' JJ spits.

'And you don't know anything about me either!' she sneers back.

I'm thankful as I see Dad pull up along the pavement, and quickly usher my friends down the steps and into the car. I feel JJ shrink back beside me and I know he must be worried about losing control. To our relief, Vicky calls shotgun and climbs up front. I smile as I watch JJ struggle with the seatbelt for a moment, then feel that strange spark between us once again as I reach out to help him and our fingers brush.

There's a stretch of awkward silence for the duration of the drive, mostly filled by Vicky flipping through the tracks on the CD player. Dad is far too polite to say anything - Vicky has been around our family since we came to Fortune's Well. We're all a little too used to her ways by now.

JJ's hand is on the middle seat next to mine. So close, I could just move mine about half an inch and - *Oh shit...* I did it. It feels like the entire world has stopped, then I feel his fingers wrap around mine and squeeze. I can't look up at him, but I know he must be looking at me.

'So, what happened tonight?' he whispers.

'I told you, I just fainted. It was no big deal.'

'I meant between you and the *She Devil.*' He nods towards the front seat. 'But we can talk about the other thing too… if you want. You can talk to me about anything.' His grip tightens, then, as if remembering himself his face grows serious and he leans away.

'I… I'm not ready to talk about it yet… the *other* thing,' I whisper.

'Okay.'

'As for Vicky, I really don't think she's as bad as you say. She might blab if she finds out… but maybe, if it comes to that, I could speak to her and…'

We are on the road to the farm now and in his eyes soft swirls of mist flood his pupils. He blinks them away. *That's new.*

'JJ, your eyes they… I think it's time. It's time you speak to your mother. Whatever it takes. I'll go with you if you want?'

JJ nods, his expression grim. 'I know, but it's Uncle Henry. He won't let me. We'll have to find another way.'

'How? I can keep researching but we're running out of time. What you did tonight to Andrew and Frankie… You're losing control.'

'You're a fine one to talk!' His words are cutting, and his eyes are deep, black holes once again. He rubs his temples and winces. 'Sorry, I don't know what's happening to me.'

'It's okay,' I reassure him but deep down I know it's not.

*

As we pull up to the house, Henry Carson looms in the doorway. Before my dad cuts the headlights, I can't help but notice the flush of pink in his face. He's clearly been drinking. I have to say something - the way JJ's been we can't just leave him here to explode again. Before I can speak, everyone has removed their seatbelts and climbed from the car.

'What trouble you got yourself in now?' Henry slurs.

JJ shoves past him and storms up the stairs.

'Mr Carson, there's some things we didn't get to discuss on the phone earlier. Do you mind?' My dad gestures towards the hallway and Henry moves aside. I follow with Vicky in tow.

'Hello again…' She winks at Henry. He looks back at her like he's going to puke, and not just from the alcohol.

There's a banging from upstairs and I follow it, all the way up to JJ's room. He's sitting on the end of the bed with his head in his hands. I perch next to him and Vicky slithers into the room behind me.

'Hey, are you okay?'

'What the fuck is your dad doing? He's going to piss off Uncle Henry, and I already have too much to deal with… Can you not touch that!'

Vicky places a book back onto the bedside table and throws me a look.

'JJ, my dad just wants to help.'

'He does? Is that *really* what you think?'

My mind floods will all the memories of the computer and the strange way my dad has been acting recently. 'Well, actually…'

164

'I should go check on them. Uncle Henry can get very… *unstable*… when he's had a drink.' He stalks out of the room, taking a record from Vicky's hands and placing it back on the pile. She walks over to the window and sighs.

'So, here we are, babes. The freak's lair.'

'I told you already, don't call him that.'

'Wow. You really have a thing for him, don't you?'

'We're just friends.'

'That's not an answer, DeeDee.' She picks up a box on the windowsill, it jingles as if it's full of broken china or glass. She rolls it around in her hands. 'You really left Ben for this guy?'

'It's not like that… JJ is… *special.*'

'Sounds serious.'

'Honestly, Vick. If you just got to know him, you'd see he isn't that bad.'

'Never gonna happen, babes. But listen, if you're happy. I guess I can like… try an' be less of a bitch to him. Maybe a little. I still don't trust the freak though.' I shoot her a death stare. '*Kid*. I still don't trust the kid.' She corrects herself.

'What the fuck are you doing!?' JJ bursts through the door, fists clenched in his hair.

'JJ, calm down… We were jus-'

'I said what are you doing!? Put that down!'

'JJ!'

'I told you not to touch my shit!' He storms across the room and snatches the box from Vicky. She rears back and steps towards me, grabbing my arm.

'I… I was only…'

'JJ, you need to *stop*!' The mist is swirling around his wrists and growing thicker, darker.

'Just get out, Darcie. Just get the hell out!' A stream of mist hits me hard in the chest, knocking the wind right out of me. It freezes the skin beneath my shirt, causing a dull ache like a bruise.

'I told you he was a *freak*!' Vicky squeals, unhelpfully.

I'm staring at JJ and there they are again, those cold, dark eyes. He begins to shake, his hands scrunched into fists. I grab Vicky's arm and storm out of the room. My insides are screaming out for me to help him, to try and keep him calm. But my head tells me there is nothing I can do for him now. The best thing I can do is get Vicky as far away from him as possible.

'Sweetheart, what-'

'We'll be in the car, Dad.' We race out the door and climb into the backseats. As I pull on my seatbelt a shadow in the upstairs window catches my eye. I look up, lip trembling, already aware of what I am going to see. Sure enough, there it is. The huge hulking silhouette of the hangman pressing up against the glass.

29: JJ

I watch the car drive away and turn around, my shoulders suddenly hunched and tense, like someone has walked over my grave. I feel a shudder, almost a jolt and think I see something dark and human-shaped looming over me, but then it's gone, and it's just me, with my bandaged-up hand and my burning resentment. Vicky Marshall. *Christ*, it's like everything is unravelling and it's all her fault. How can Darcie and I get to the truth with her hanging around like a bad smell? She can't be trusted, surely Darcie realises this?

Anger settles in my bones making me feel cold and hard. I lower my head and it's like all my thoughts and feelings scatter in fear, making way for something fiercer, something primal and old. I stalk quickly towards the door. I don't know where I am going or what I am going to do but I've had enough. No one *ever* gets what they deserve around here! It's about time some people started to pay...

I wrench open my door and walk straight into Uncle Henry's fist. It's like a rock coming for me and there is no time to duck or dive. It collides with my face and everything goes black before I even hit the floor.

*

When I come to, I'm slumped against my bedroom wall and a groggy head turn reveals that Uncle Henry is slumped next to me. He is holding a pack of frozen peas against my right eye which feels heavy and swollen. There is a dull, throbbing ache behind the peas and when I lift a hand to wipe my nose it comes away with fresh blood smeared across my knuckles.

'That wasn't me,' grunts Uncle Henry. 'That just started. Your nose is like a bloody tap. Here.' He shoves a handful of scrunched up tissues at me and I take them from him and press them against my leaking nostrils.

I stare at the floor, confused and afraid and ridiculously tired again, and I see a shoe box sitting next to my leg. My mouth hangs open as I frown at it, not understanding.

Uncle Henry pulls up his legs and wraps one chunky arm around them. He is watching me carefully but I can't look at him. Last time I saw him I shoved him into the wall with the mist and now he's smacked me back. Where the hell can we go from here? Silently, I start to cry.

He shifts his weight towards me, gently pulls back the pack of peas and winces at whatever he sees underneath. 'That wasn't because you shoved me,' he says, lifting my hand and easing it into place to hold the pack. 'Keep it like that.'

'What was it for then?' I ask, and my voice comes out small and thin and dull with shock.

'That was for getting that stuck-up prick Duffield to threaten me,' Uncle Henry says, and when I look at him, he raises his eyebrows at me, nods once and then gazes away. 'Yeah, he's taken a real shine to you, eh?' He loops his other arm around his knees and stares hard at the floor. 'That's a good thing, I suppose, what with you hanging around his precious daughter. But you know, I could do without being threatened in my own front yard and I could do without interfering know-it-all's like him telling me what to do.'

I don't understand any of this. I lower the tissues and wrinkle my nose. The blood seems to have stopped, so that's something. 'He threatened you? Why?'

'He said I've got no right to stop you seeing your mum. He said he can provide legal help to you if I continue to stop you seeing her.' Uncle Henry lifts his big broad shoulders and then drops them with a short exhale of weary breath. 'Threatened me with all sorts, if you want to know the truth. Accused me of being *neglectful*. He can accuse me of a lot worse now, can't he?'

I lower the pack of peas and blink my eye gingerly. I can just about see out of it and anyway, I figure I deserve it for shoving him like that. I look around for my glasses and Uncle Henry hands them to me.

'I won't tell him,' I mutter, my head low. 'I'm sorry, Uncle Henry. I'm sorry for yelling and shoving you. I don't know what happened.'

'Neither do I,' he sighs. 'But Duffield is right about one thing. I got no right keeping you from your mum. If you need to see her, you need to see her. I won't stand in your way, JJ.'

I nod in thanks. 'What's in the box?'

'Ah,' he reaches for the box, dragging it towards him. He flips off the lid with one thumb. 'Your mum put this together before she went to prison. She begged me to give it to you when you were old enough. I nearly burned it to be honest. Few times over the years I've come close to throwing it out but anyway… It's for you.'

I'm not sure I want to look inside it. I remember the jar and think how leaving it empty was the start of all this craziness, so why would I want anything else from her? But then I wonder, *was* it the jar? Or was all of this in motion long before that? I think back to my drawings and how even years ago I would see this kind of swirling grey smoke on the page, like another pencil directing mine, urging me to see what it wanted me to see. I always told myself it was my vivid imagination at work and once I had finished the drawing, it would go away and I would feel better.

He pushes the box towards me and I peer into it, my breath caught in my throat as tears continue to fill my eyes. I cough and reach in. The item on the top is pale blue and unbelievably soft. As soon as my fingers make contact, I want to pick it up and lay it against my cheek. It's a small square of material and I turn it over in my hands in wonder.

'Your baby blanky,' Uncle Henry murmurs beside me. 'You were surgically attached to that thing, you know. It was always gross and covered in shit and food and dribble. You loved it.'

'I don't remember it.'

'Nah, you grew out of it around three or four, I think. Guess she hung on to it. James used to tell me she'd stuff it in a glass jar sometimes and he thought she was odd, doing that with a bit of old cloth. Not the only odd thing about her, I guess, but anyway.'

I lay it on my knee and pick up the next item. It's a tiny baby vest, one of those all-in-one things that has poppers between the legs. It's white with a tiny blue sailing boat embroidered on the chest.

'First thing you ever wore,' says Uncle Henry. 'Course it was too big for you because you were a right scrawny little thing.'

I laugh a little and lay it next to the piece of blue cloth. 'Can't believe she kept all this.'

'Mothers keep a lot of weird stuff,' he grunts.

The next thing I pick up is a tiny glass bottle with a metal screw-on lid. Inside, staring back at me are a number of tiny teeth. 'Oh yuk,' I exclaim as Henry chuckles. 'That *is* weird. I guess the tooth fairy isn't real then, hey?'

'About as real as Father Christmas,' he replies.

The next item is a rolled-up piece of paper. I pull off the rubber band and unroll it to see my birth certificate. My heart feels weak and shuddery, my sobs hitched and trapped in my throat as I scan the paper and see all our names. Mother - Cora Bridget Carson. Occupation – artist. Father - James John Carson. Occupation - farmer. And me, JJ Carson, named after my father.

'Wow.' I blink back tears and quickly wipe my eyes with the back of one hand. 'It's weird, seeing their names there like that.' I look at my uncle and I long to ask him a thousand questions about my parents but all I can do is stare.

He swallows and lowers his eyes with a brief nod. 'I didn't always hate her, you know.'

This is news to me. 'You didn't?'

'No. In fact, when they first started going out, I thought she was too good for my brother.'

Wow, really? 'I had no idea,' I whisper.

'They met at a stupid dance, can you believe that?' A slight grin lifts his lips and brightens his eyes. 'They don't do it anymore but they used to have these cheesy dances at the community hall for us kids. Cora was a year younger than James so they hadn't mixed at school. They met there. I think she was in awe of him… she hung on his every word. I mean, all the girls did. James was…' Uncle Henry trails off then clears his throat, his expression darkening again. 'He didn't always treat her right, I guess. But anyway,' he clears his throat again and nods at the certificate. 'I figured at least that might be handy. Keep looking.'

I pull the box onto my lap. There are a few more baby things. A battered little wooden train which I think I vaguely remember. A scrap of paper with a scrawled stick man on it. One of my early drawings, I guess. A lock of blonde hair inside an envelope and a pair of tiny brown trainers which must have been the first shoes I ever wore.

And at the bottom is a large brown envelope. I take it out and my heart speeds up again, almost as if it knows something is up. My mouth grows dry and my fingers tremble as I pick it up, open it and slide out the paperwork inside. For a few moments I flick through it, scanning my eyes over the words, all written in official legal language. I'm not too sure, but I think I am looking at the deeds to Hangman's Cottage and they are in my name.

I turn to Uncle Henry and maybe my face has gone pale or something, because he suddenly looks concerned and he takes the paperwork from me and starts folding it up and sliding it back into the envelope.

'I don't understand.'

He scratches his cheek, not looking at me. 'It's simple, JJ. The house is yours, the cottage. It's been in your mother's family for generations and I'm not gonna lie, I thought about throwing this all out because I knew this was in there and I don't want you to have it JJ, I don't want that house to be yours.'

My lips feel like paper as I ask him, 'It's mine?'

'When you turn eighteen,' he nods, swallowing hard, not looking at me still. 'That's what it does, see? It passes along, from one generation to the next, just like… just like…' He trails off and shakes his head and looks like he is about to get up and walk out.

I reach for his knee and grab it. 'Like what? Like whatever was wrong with them all? My mum and her mum and the rest? It's something to do with the cottage, isn't it? There's something wrong with that place?'

He shrugs, still shaking his head while panic runs wild in his eyes. 'I don't know. JJ, I don't goddamn know, if it's the bloody cottage or just that bloody family, but you wanted to know, so now you know and if you want to know any more, you'll have to go and see her and get it from her.'

He pulls away from my hand and gets up on shaky legs. He passes me back the envelope and I drop it quickly into the shoe box. Panicking, feeling on edge, I start to pile the baby things back on top so that I can forget it was ever there.

'You want my advice?' he says from above. I look up at him, waiting. 'You go see her. You tell her everything, anything you want, you be honest with her JJ, and honest with yourself and then you come back here with me and try your goddamn hardest *not* to be like them, you hear me? And when you're eighteen you sell that godforsaken creepy, cursed old cottage and finally be free. You do all that...' he nods at me firmly. 'And you and me stand a chance.'

30: Darcie

'No, no, no, go back!'

'I can't move!'

'You have to go back... Now!'

'I'm stuck... Help me!'

'No, just listen, you have to-Ugh! We were so close to level ten!'

Jeremy slumps back onto his bed with a huff.

'Wanna go again?'

'Nah, it's okay. What happened? You slayed at this last time we played.'

'I guess I just... Never mind.'

My stomach growls as I climb to my feet, and I am painfully aware of the fact that I haven't had anything to eat since the episode in the en suite. I would murder a cheeseburger right now. The word *murder* makes me quiver as I recall the figure looming in JJ's window watching me. What did it want? Is this all because of me? First, I'd seen it in the cottage and then tonight... Does it know that I'm trying to protect JJ from his power? Is it trying to scare the shit out of me to silence me for good? Well, it can fucking try. But I won't give up. I'm smart enough to give JJ his space and allow him to calm down, but I will keep searching for answers. If I don't, who else does he have? And why the hell am I the only one that can see what's happening to him?

'Earth to Darcie. Hello. Are you in there?'

'Huh?'

'You totally spaced for like a minute.'

'Sorry. Head injury.' I tap my temple then wince as the pain shoots through my eye socket. *Big mistake.*

'You okay?' My brother jumps from his bed and runs over to steady me, but I shrug him off with a laugh.

'I'll live.' *I hope.*

Jeremy sighs once more and it looks as if he's going to say something, but he stops himself. The words hovering on the tip of his tongue. I decide to shatter the silence.

'You know earlier, in the hallway. You were talking about Dad and-'

'I don't want to talk about it.'

'Well, when you do…'

He flashes me a grin.

'I'm gonna go grab some ice cream. I'm starved. You want anything?'

'Nah I'm good.'

'Okay… Remember, Jer. Anytime.'

'I know.'

*

The hit of sticky sweetness feels soothing on my tongue as I suck on the end of the spoon. I lift the tub and place it against my forehead. *Ah, even better.*

'You're up late.' My mother wades into the kitchen, her hair wild and a fluffy dressing gown tied tightly around her waist. It's a rare sight indeed, to see her this way. Unpolished. Normal. 'You'll be tired tomorrow.'

'I'm not five anymore.'

'I know.' Her eyes fall on the tub in front of me and I automatically place the lid back onto it. Mom grabs a spoon from the drawer and slides into the seat opposite. I gawk at her. 'Are you not going to share?' she asks, and I slide the tub across the counter. 'Ah, mint chocolate chip. You've always loved this one.' She gouges out a chunk with her spoon and places it into her mouth before sighing with satisfaction. 'Mmm, so good.' She nods towards the tub and unsure of exactly what is happening, I lift my own spoon and we begin fighting over scoops.

'Not exactly foie gras, right?'

I laugh. 'No, but much better.'

'Sorry about earlier, sweetheart. Leaving you in the hospital like that.'

'Oh, it's okay.'

'No, it's really not.' She places her spoon on the counter and rests her chin in her hand. 'Julia and I went to grab a coffee after we collected your brother from Christopher's, we thought we'd give you some time to rest up. Then your father called me, said he had that friend of yours in the car with him and that they were on their way to the hospital.'

'Makes sense, Mom.' There's something about her expression, like a light fading out, that causes me to put down my spoon. 'Mom?'

'Oh sweetheart, the truth is I was glad when your father called. I was feeling so bloody angry and it gave me an excuse to get out.'

'Angry? Because of what Doctor Fisher said? Mom you don't-'

'Angry with myself.'

There are tears brimming in her eyes, but she doesn't brush them away or hide them. She embraces her pain and allows them to roll down her cheeks. Mine do the same, leaving a salty taste on my lips. She reaches across and brushes the hair from my face.

'I was angry because Doctor Fisher was right about me. I have been neglecting you. She could see it, Julia could see it, I was probably the only one that couldn't.' She gazes away, chewing at her lip.

'Mom…'

'Shush, you need to hear this.'

I reach out and grab hold of her hand. I clasp it so tightly, as if it will fizzle away into nothing if I even consider letting go.

'I know I haven't been the perfect mother. I've made a lot of mistakes. But just know that everything I have ever done has been because I love you Darcie. I only ever want what's best for you. You always were a daddy's girl, and we… We've never had anything in common. Our hair. Our eyes. Our taste in music. We're just so different and I got scared Darcie, I got so bloody scared…' Her fingers grip mine tightly. 'I got scared that once you realised we were so different that you wouldn't love me anymore. You wouldn't want me in your life. So, I tried to push you to do things with me, dinner parties, get into a good college. I just wanted to feel like we had something, some connection. I see now that I've pushed you too far. I am so, so sorry my darling.'

'I love you, Mom.' I release her hand, move around the counter and wrap my arms around her.

'I love you too, darling. More than you'll ever know.' There's a cosiness between us, like being wrapped in a big blanket during a rainstorm. 'Now, come on, off to bed.' She pats my arm and breaks away. 'You'll waste the day away tomorrow otherwise.'

'Mom, I'm not-'

'Five anymore, so I hear. But no matter what, you'll always be my little girl.'

*

I nestle into the warmth of the duvet, a smile spreading across my face. For the first time in what feels like years, I feel safe, and loved, and happy. I feel like a little girl again. The mirror across the way is blank, and it's nice to know the girl has given me the night off. Tonight, I can simply be alone without the constant nagging feeling in my gut and my head so full of questions. As I drift off, something scurries across the floor and away into the shadows. I squint into the darkness and wait for it to reappear. When it doesn't, I decide that I must be imagining things. It has been a crazy few days.

Then I see her. Vicky Marshall, staggering out from behind the curtains. Hair drenched. Face caked in mud. Her arms are bare and she's shivering. Her eyes are darting all around.

'Vicky?' She can't hear me. She walks right up to the mirror and right through the glass. I throw back the covers and run towards it, place my palms against the surface and peer into it. But there's no Vicky in sight. Just deep, endless black. Until suddenly she re-emerges, flinging herself against the glass and screaming out for help. She bangs her hands against it over and over. Eyes wide with fear. Then I see him, the hangman. I let out a scream and begin clawing at the glass with my fingernails but there's nothing I can do. He's got her by the throat, squeezing tightly until her face turns blue and the glass fogs over in a thick black mist.

I continue to bang against the mirror, sobbing as I call out for my friend until I realise that there's nothing I can do, she's gone. I place my forehead against the glass, my ragged breath the only sound, until the hooded face appears once more from the gloom, staring right back at me before slipping away. As my eyes adjust to the darkness,

178

the reflection of the room behind me comes into view and I slide my body down to the floor, shaking.

31: JJ

A few days after Mr Duffield threatened Uncle Henry, I'm sitting in the family room waiting for my mother to appear. It's a large, spacious room, with big windows letting warm sunlight stream across the dusky green carpet. The walls are painted a calming sea blue and are decorated with various amateur prints I'm guessing either the inmates or their children painted. I'm nervous - shitting myself, actually. I've bitten my nails down to nothing and I can't stop jiggling my knees up and down. Thankfully, there is no sign of the mist and there hasn't been since me and Uncle Henry had our chat.

I still can't believe he gave me that box and let me see my mum. He's always been so against me seeing her; always used any excuse he could find to stop me going and a lot of times I went along with that, partly to please him and partly because I was scared to see her. The visits have become scarcer over the last few years. I think it's been six months since I last saw her and I feel horribly guilty.

I know what she did was bad but she's stuck in here all alone with nothing but time on her hands. I'm all she has in the world and I've been shutting her out to please Uncle Henry. But that's okay, now I'm here I can try to explain that to her. I can say I'm sorry. And I can ask her about the cottage and her family and the mist.

I drop my head, close my eyes and breathe in deeply, trying like hell to calm my shaky nerves. The door opens suddenly without warning, making me jump in alarm and she walks right in. She's smaller than I remember. Or have I grown? She seems to think so as her eyes widen and her mouth falls open in surprise and joy. I stand up awkwardly, not knowing what to do, or say, or how to act.

'JJ, oh my God…' she reaches for me, closing the distance between us in seconds and wrapping her thin arms tightly around me. There are two nurses behind her, both dressed in white, one smiling, one blank faced.

'We'll be right outside the door, Cora,' the smiling one says before gently shushing the door closed. I stare over her shoulder and can see both nurses through the glass window of the door. My mother has never committed another violent act since she killed my father, not to herself or anyone else so they consider her low risk these days.

She grasps my hand and pulls me over to the low, squashy sofa I was just sitting on. 'How are you?' she gushes, clinging to my hand and leaning over her knees to gaze intently into my face. 'It is *so* good to see you!'

'Yeah, I'm okay,' I nod hesitantly. 'I'm sorry I haven't been in for so long. It was Uncle Henry…he was getting funny about it.'

To this, she raises her eyebrows and rolls her eyes, but the smile remains on her face. 'I imagine he was. Don't worry, JJ. I understand. You've grown taller!' She lifts a hand and gently caresses my cheek. 'You're getting so handsome too. How are you? How is school and everything? What have you been up to?'

'It's okay,' I say, which is obviously a lie, but I am conscious of how little time we might have together and how important it is I get what I came for. 'Mum, listen, I need to talk to you. There's stuff I really need to ask you. Is that okay?'

'What happened to your eye?' she frowns then, turning my face to hers.

'Nothing, it's not important. Mum, lots of weird stuff has been happening and I can't talk to anyone else or they're gonna think I'm crazy like…' I bite my lip and stop myself in time but she just grins and wrinkles her nose up at me.

'Like me?' she laughs and I gaze at my knees.

'I'm sorry, that's not what I meant.'

'It is, let's be honest,' she says, her hands entwined with mine again on top of my knee. 'And I don't mind, really. Look where I am. Look what I did. Those are facts, JJ, we can't run away from them. Now what's been happening? What weird stuff?'

Oh God, where do I begin?

'I don't know where to start...' I lift my eyes and gaze slowly around the room we are confined to. I suddenly want to ask her everything. Why did she do it? Why did she wreck everything? Isn't it all her fault that she's in here and my dad is dead and I am totally unwanted? I feel the anger rush through me and check my hands. Sure enough, there are tendrils emerging softly from my fingertips. I close my hands into fists and they remain buried under my tight grip. Why does it only happen when I'm angry? What does that mean?

'Start with what you need to ask me,' Mum suggests, shaking back her hair. She smiles when I catch her eye. 'Take your time. Take a deep breath. You feel cold, JJ. Your hands are freezing...Please tell me what's wrong.'

'I think I'm like you,' I mumble. There, I said it. Spat it out as simply and quickly as I could. I side-eye her and she is frowning heavily at me, her eyes narrowed down.

'Like me how?'

'Like you...weird,' I shrug, sorry that it comes out so rude but unable to think of any other way to word it. 'Freaky,' I add. 'Crazy. Dangerous. Uncle Henry thinks so too. Everyone looks at me funny. And I feel funny, Mum, I feel wrong.'

'In what way?' she questions, peering closer as my head drops lower. 'Give me an example.'

'An example?'

'Yeah, did you do something? Did you hurt someone?'

I remember Jared Wheeler in the public toilet - his face as I punched him again and again and the sound of his skull cracking against the sink. I suck in air and release it shakily.

'Yes,' I tell her. 'I hurt someone. He was hurting my friend and I stepped in but I went too far. He's okay and no one knows but... I'm scared. Is there something wrong with me too?'

'That sounds pretty normal to me,' she says, squeezing my hand.

'No,' I shake my head firmly. 'It wasn't. It *isn't* normal. Mum, if I got mad enough, I could pick you up and throw you across this room.'

'Okay,' she says, leaning even closer. 'You need to keep your voice down, honey. What are you talking about?'

'Powers, or something,' I shrug, miserably. 'I think it's been there for a while but lately it's got worse, I mean, it's got more powerful. I can do things, Mum. I can really hurt people if I want to.' I meet her eye and ask the question I have never been brave enough to ask until now. 'Was that what happened to you? The day you killed Dad?'

My mother's hold on my hands loosens and she sinks back into the sofa. It's as if all the life in her slowly seeps out and when I turn to look, she seems pale and deflated.

'I suppose I always knew you'd ask me,' she murmurs.

'Well, yeah. I've always been afraid to, but I deserve to know, don't I?'

She nods, but looks unconvinced, her hands now slack in her lap and her eyes fixed on the wall in front.

'Mum?' I prompt after a few minutes pass by. 'Are you gonna tell me?'

She sighs and a slight smile lifts her lips. 'He was cheating you know.'

I press my hands together, squeezing the faint wisps of miss between my palms. 'I know that's what you said.'

'It was true. It had been going on for a year or so… An old friend of his. I think he got itchy feet, got bored, I don't know. Maybe he loved her. I don't know. But it was true because I saw it.'

'You caught them?'

'No, I saw them in my head,' she meets my eye and smiles gently. 'You say you have this power, JJ? You can hurt people if you want to? Well, with me, it was a sort of vivid knowing, I guess. For instance, when I asked what happened to your eye, I was pretending I didn't already know.'

'What?'

'Henry did it,' she says with certainty. 'Because someone threatened him. That's why you're here as well, because Henry was forced. He's never hit you before, I know that. And I'm sure he feels bad.'

My mind is in utter turmoil. What the hell is she talking about? 'What are you saying, you can predict the future?'

'No, not the future' she shakes her head and laughs at the suggestion. 'I can just see. Like now, I'm looking at you and I know that you were in a hospital yesterday.' She bites her lips and narrows her eyes as she stares at me intensely. 'You hurt your hand. You curled up on a bed and fell asleep. And… and I can see you in your room too, at Henry's. This must be after he hit you because your eye is swollen. Then he gave you my box?' Her eyes widen and a bright smile fills her face.

I nod. 'Yeah, he did. So you can see what I've been doing, without me telling you?'

'Yes, that's it. And with your father he'd come home from work and I'd see images in my head of where he had really been. He'd hold me and kiss me and I'd see her in my head. I could even smell her.'

'That's amazing…' I mumble.

My mother claps her hands between her knees and sits forward again. 'I had it when I was little but it was much weaker then,' she tells me. 'And of course I didn't know what it was, or even that it was unusual until I was much older and somehow my mother must have realised. By then, I think I was a bit younger than you, it was making me really sad.'

'Sad?'

'Yeah, sad. Terribly, awfully sad. Of course, the school were worried and suggested my mum take me to the doctor so she did and of course, they wanted to put me on anti-depressants. My mother pretended to go along with it all but when she got me home, she sat me down and told me the truth.'

I shift to face her better. 'What truth?'

'The same truth I better tell you, JJ.' She sucks in her breath then bites her lower lip while her bright blue eyes burn into me. 'You need to know,' she whispers, 'you need to know what is happening to you and why. You need to know what happened that day between me and your father.'

I swallow the hard lump in my throat and my eyes are stinging with unshed tears. I force myself to nod, to give her permission to go on but I am cold and frightened. I am terrified of what she is about to tell me.

32: Darcie

The waiting room reeks with the sickly-sweet scent of potpourri. It infiltrates my nostrils and causes my head to spin. The walls are lined with vintage style chairs, all high wooden backs and garish cushions. On the far wall a clock ticks away obnoxiously, yet its hands never seem to move from the same position. I reach out for one of the magazines on the small circular table in the centre of the room. *All crap.* I lean back against the hard seat with a huff. There's a clunking noise as a door handle lowers and a tall, thin woman emerges.

'Miss Duffield.'

With a grin I climb to my feet and follow her into her office. Ever since that talk with my mother the other night, things are a lot more positive at home. But I would be a fool to think that all my problems would fizzle away overnight. My parents had, for once, thought about me, and I mean *really* thought about me for a change. They'd thought about me so much that they decided it would be best that I make an appointment with a counsellor, Doctor Nicola, and who knows? Maybe this is the right thing for me after all…

'Take a seat.' She gestures to a chair opposite her desk and to my horror its near identical to the torture device I had just spent twenty-five minutes sat on in the waiting area. 'So, Miss Duffield, do you mind if I call you Darcie?'

I grunt a reply.

'Well then Darcie, how are you feeling today?'

'Good.'

'Good?'

'Yeah… Good.'

'That's good.'

'Yeah...'

She bites her lip as she scribbles hurriedly on her notepad. The scratching of the nib against the paper seems to drag on longer than that damn clock in the waiting room. She leans back in her chair, the pleather squeaking against her body. One solitary kitten heel taps against the hardwood flooring. My fingers twitch and my sweater suddenly becomes unbearably itchy. *Why did I agree to this again?*

'Now, Darcie, I know a little about why you are here, but why don't you tell me again, in your own words. What brings you here today?'

'Um... My parents thought-'

'Your parents? What about you?'

'I have an issue with eating.' The words spill out of me. It feels freeing but also unnatural. I don't know if I'm ready for this, if I'm ready to be here, talking.

'When you say *issue*,' she clears her throat and shifts in her seat. 'What is your relationship like with food?'

'My relationship?'

'Do you avoid eating entirely, binge eat, or...?'

'Both I guess.'

'Hmm...' Again, with the scratching on the pad. 'What is it you think makes you feel this way? Are you under any kind of pressure at all?' I consider this for a moment before nodding. It's no secret to me that I am always being pushed and pulled in so many directions. In fact, it is slowly starting to feel less weird, opening up to an adult like this. 'Must be tough,' she sighs as she scribbles down another note, 'being a Duffield.' She catches my expression and gives me a knowing smile. Flipping her notepad shut she places it on the desk and she shuffles her chair a little closer, hands clasped together in her lap.

'Your father has always been an over achiever, and Alyssa is quite the social climber.'

'You… You know my parents?'

'Oh, yes Darcie, we go way back. But don't worry, this is all entirely confidential. They won't hear a peep about anything we discuss, oh no.' She flashes a warm smile and something in her eyes tells me I can trust her.

'But I don't understand. We only moved here when I was twelve.'

'I spent entire summers with Malcolm. Down by the river. Not just him and I of course! Oh no, nothing like that. He'd often come over with the family to visit his aunt.'

'Aunt?'

'Yes. Speaking of aunts, may I just say I always loved Jenna Duffield. She was such a fearless little thing. I was so saddened to hear she had passed.'

'Sorry, but I don't understand… Dad's family are from Orange County. Mom was born in England, but she doesn't have any family left.'

'Oh no, Darcie. Your father had family right here in Fortune's Well.'

'Fortune's Well…' The words leave my lips in a whisper.

'Anyway, Darcie. We digress. You were just telling me abou-'

'I don't wanna talk about that.' She recoils and the pleather squeaks. 'I just… Can we talk about something else?'

'The hour is yours. We can talk about whatever you like.'

My fingers weave in and out of one another as I peer across the row of photographs on the shelf behind her head. There's a large brass frame in the centre with an image of three beaming boys. One of them I am pretty sure I recognise somehow… Perhaps from school… He looks so familiar, but I can't quite place him… He's much younger in this photo than he would be now. His round face is framed by light hair which is swept into curtains, he has one tooth missing, and he's wearing a bright blue Superman t-shirt. My mind turns to JJ Carson.

'You said anything I say in here is confidential, right?'

'Absolutely, yes. Unless I feel you're a danger to yourself or someone else, I can't discuss whatever you tell me with anyone.' She smiles at me once more, but this time concern masks her eyes.

'Do you believe some people are… *special?*'

'Well, I suppose every one of us is special in our own way.'

'No, I mean, do you believe we can have *powers?* Like superheroes do. Something we can't explain, or even tell anybody about.'

'We've all got things about us. Secret identities we feel we cannot share. It's all perfectly normal.' She reaches across to the desk then hands me a few flyers.

'Oh, I'm not gay Doctor Nicola,' I flush, handing them back to her. Her left eyebrow raises ever so slightly as she observes me with disbelief, then places them back onto the desk.

'I don't even know what I'm trying to say.'

'That's okay, take your time.'

I take a breath. 'A friend of mine, strange things have been happening… Dark clouds. And there's these visions, creepy figures. A girl trapped inside the mirror.'

'Ah,' She leans forwards once more with a grin. 'I think I follow. You know, having hallucinations could be linked to lack of nutrition. Your friend in the mirror… I think sometimes we can project what we are feeling as a way of processing strong emotion or trauma. Especially as young women. We're bombarded by ideas of how our body should look. I think it would be great if we could come up with a meal plan together and help change your relationship with food, whilst working through your troubles of course. As a team.'

I don't know what else to say or do, so I just sit there and smile. How the heck am I ever going to understand what is happening to JJ and myself if I can't find anyone to communicate with? Man, I wish Jenna was here for this. She'd understand. I just know it.

The rest of the hour passes much the same. Me awkwardly dodging questions and feeling increasingly uncomfortable in my skin. Every time there is a flicker of hope for a breakthrough, Doctor Nicola says something else that makes me feel entirely misunderstood. Then she pulls a wad of flimsy plastic cards out from her drawer and holds them up in front of me.

I've seen this done in movies but didn't know it was an actual thing. Each card has a random coloured spot on it, and you have to say what you see. But all I see is murky green smudges and red splatters like blood. Then comes the final card, a burning orange heart shape painted in the centre. I look into it and my own heart skips a beat, because there's only one thing I can see staring right back at me from it—the face of JJ Carson.

33: JJ

'That was the day I knew for sure,' my mother says, tucking her dark blonde hair behind her ears and biting anxiously at her lower lip. Her hands are now pressed together between her knees, which are trembling slightly. Her eyes are mostly fixed on the carpet but every now and then they swivel to take me in, to judge my reaction. 'He came home, smelling of her. You were at a friend's house having tea. He was late home, throwing excuses at me as he rolled in, barely looking at me. And I could see it, JJ. I could see it all in my head just like I had for years.'

'What did you see?' I ask, my voice barely above a croak.

'James and the woman he'd been with,' she replies, eyes down again. 'In bed. I don't need to go into the details. But that wasn't the worst of it. I could see that he intended to leave me. He was torn between us - that's what I saw, but he couldn't bear the lies anymore, the double life, so he was going to leave me. Leave us. I saw red, I guess. Flew into a rage.'

'What happened?'

'He was in the bedroom, pulling off his boots. He threw one behind him. He always did stuff like that, just threw his stuff everywhere expecting me to pick it up without complaint. Anyway, it hit the bedside table on my side of the bed, which was where I kept my mother's jar.'

My spine uncurls with a jolt, my head shoots up and my eyes grow wide. The jar? This can't have all been to do with that bloody jar? 'The one you gave me?'

'Yes, the one my mother gave me and her mother gave her.'

'It's not magic,' I whisper, staring at her. 'It can't be.'

She meets my eye and smiles in pity. 'And yet you're telling me you have superhero style powers that can throw people across rooms? JJ, *anything* is possible.'

'He knocked the jar over?' I ask, barely breathing now.

She nods. 'Knocked it over, knocked out the little drawing you'd done the day before. I was always putting new things in the jar, you see, just like my mother warned me to. And it worked,' she unclasps her hands and turns them palms up for a second, before sinking them back between her knees. 'It worked for years, as long as I kept it full of anything that made me happy. I could still see stuff that had happened but it was okay. I could handle it. I was me.'

'I don't understand. What happened when the jar got knocked over?'

'It was a bad moment,' Mum says, licking her lips as her eyes return to bore holes into the carpet. 'I think on any other day, I would have just picked it up and filled it again and it would have been okay. But it's like the darkness, the emptiness my mother always warned me about, it was there that day, waiting for me. Waiting in the room. And I guess it seized an opportunity JJ, me knowing James was going to leave us, me seeing him in bed with that other woman and not being able to prove any of it. And there was a hammer on the windowsill where I had a framed picture I wanted to hang up. Another one of yours. And I'd been asking James for weeks to hang it for me because I could never get them straight.'

I hold up a hand and shift slightly away from her. She takes the cue and stops talking and a dark silence falls over us both. I chew at my ragged nails. I don't need her to tell me what happened next because I can work it out for myself. Whatever it was, the darkness, the emptiness, the curse, whatever we call it, it saw its chance and got into her, just like it got into me when I stopped Jared hurting Darcie. And she picked up the hammer and killed him. And she got sent away, probably forever, and Uncle Henry had to take me on, even though he was grieving his brother and every time he looked at me, he saw her, the killer, staring right back at him. We never stood a chance.

But what is it? Where did it come from? How can we stop the same thing happening to me? Suddenly, I think about Darcie and my head fills up with her face and her hair and her tough, sassy attitude, and my heart fills up so badly it becomes an unbearable physical ache. I can trust her. She can help me. She *wants* to help me.

I swallow and shift back to look at my mother. She is staring at the floor, her knees shaking, her shoulders hunched and stiff.

'That's why you gave me the jar,' I say and she nods. 'But I didn't take it seriously,' I go on, 'and it was empty. And the mist, whatever it is, it got worse, it got more powerful and when it comes, Mum, I like it. I like how dark and powerful it makes me feel.'

She sniffs as a single tear wells in one eye before toppling slowly down her cheek. She reaches out, finding my knee and gripping it. 'I know,' she says, staring into my eyes, 'believe me I know how it feels. I remember. But I don't know where it came from, JJ, and I am so sorry, my love, I don't know how to get rid of it.'

'What did your mum tell you about it?'

Mum shrugs at me and palms away the single tear. 'She had some abilities, I suppose. Not like you or me. Hers was more like mind-reading. When I was little, it was wonderful. Imagine having a newborn baby screaming its head off and because you can read minds and emotions, you know exactly what is wrong with it so can fix it for them.' She breaks into a smile, so I do too. 'If I was sad, or anxious, she knew. She knew all my thoughts, all my feelings. But when I was your age, when the real sadness came, she knew it was powerful but she didn't know how to fix it.'

'Is that when she came up with the jar idea?' I ask.

Mum shakes her head. 'No, she already had that. Her mum passed it on. I honestly don't know how far back it goes, JJ, but that was when she made me try it too, yes. We used the same jar. The one you have. She would put in things that made her happy and so would I and it worked. I still had my extra sight, whatever you want to call it. I could still see things in my head, things I shouldn't have been able to see, but I could handle it, as long as the jar was full. As long as I was okay. You know?'

I shrug slightly and scratch at my neck. 'I don't know.'

'You're confused,' she sighs, dropping her head into her other hand. 'You're so young and you've had so much more to deal with than I ever did. Have you got anyone to talk to? Anyone you can trust?'

'Darcie,' I say, instantly. 'I've got Darcie. She's been helping me.'

Mum looks up and a big smile fills her face. 'Darcie. I saw her too, when you walked in. She is *so* beautiful! That's wonderful, JJ.'

I nod, unsurely. 'I hope so. I don't want to let her down or hurt her. She's my only friend, Mum and she knows everything. You know what else is weird? She's the only one who can see the mist when it happens.'

'Really? That is interesting.'

'Yeah. We went to the cottage, your mother's cottage and she saw a spirit there, I think. I didn't see anything but when we were there the mist came and it was like it attacked *me*, like it was angry at *me*…'

My mother shakes her head at me, her face creased with emotion. 'I don't know anything about the mist *or* a spirit JJ, I am so sorry.'

'It's okay,' I put my hand over hers and squeeze. 'It's not your fault. It's connected to that cottage though, Mum, it must be.'

'It was in my family for years,' she murmurs. 'But I always loved it there. I felt safe.'

'Maybe it wanted you to?'

'What do you mean it? What *it?*'

'I don't know. The hangman I guess,' I examine her face, searching for clues, but she looks genuinely blank. 'Darcie saw a figure and I drew him when she described him. I drew him exactly as she saw him, Mum. It must mean something, right? Like maybe it's a ghost or a spirit? Maybe it wants something?'

'I always thought it was just a strange name,' Mum says. 'The cottage. I mean, I guess my mother thought there had been a hangman living there at some point, because the place was so old but she didn't look into it. I don't think she knew for sure.'

'Maybe it got lost in time,' I suggest, glancing at the door. I can see the nurses out there talking, one of them reaching for the door handle. 'Forgotten through the generations? Me and Darcie will find out, Mum. She's amazing at stuff like that. We'll find the truth, I promise you.' I pick up her hand and hold it between mine. I stare into her eyes and she stares back and I think I have never seen a person look so desolate, so lost, so scared and yet so hopeful all at the same time. 'We'll figure it out,' I tell her with a nod. 'We won't let it happen again.'

34: Darcie

Sunlight spills in through the window as I run around the room, pulling on different blouses and shirts, standing in front of the mirror and adjusting the buttons up and down. Trying to find a balance between too much bra and not enough, too slutty and too Sister Margaret. Today I am meeting JJ at the library. We have so much to talk about. Last night, on my way home from the session with Doctor Nicola, I swung by the library once more. I realised I was going the wrong way about finding answers, instead of researching strange mists and demons, I should have been looking into the history of that cottage where the hangman first appeared. Sure enough, I found it—an old newspaper article with the information we needed. I text JJ immediately. I wanted to tell him there and then that we might have a breakthrough, but he replied with four short words that stopped me in my tracks: *Just seen my mum.*

I can't even imagine how he must be feeling right now. I think about my own mother and how much she annoys me at times, but to see her behind bars... I shudder. I decided instead to tell him to meet me at the library and I'd explain everything there. It's quiet, discreet and safe— exactly what we need. Besides, there was no chance of Vicky or any of Jared's goons stepping foot inside. I take one last look in the mirror with a sigh as I shift from left to right and it hits me that it doesn't matter what I look like. JJ likes me for me, just the way I am. I don't need to try with him, I don't need to be something that I'm not.

I reach into the wardrobe and pull on my favourite oversized hoodie. It's feels so fluffy and warm on the inside and the outside is black with a Guns N' Roses logo emblazoned on the front. It used to be Jenna's - there are burn holes on one sleeve from cigarette ends brushing up against her at concerts, and the hood strings are frayed at the ends. I tug at the band in my perfectly placed hair and shake out my ponytail, allowing it to spill out around me like the rays from the window. I look so rough, so dishevelled… so *me*. I smile.

As I hurry down the stairs the distinct sound of fingertips mashing against keys catches my attention. Dad must be in his office. I creep up to the door and knock, waiting for him to give me the okay to enter. My palms grow silky and a lump lodges itself to the back of my throat as I think of all the things I am going to say when I open the door.

I think of how I am going to tell him I've seen the files on his computer, how I remember that night years ago when he stopped Jenna from coming to my room. How I know we had ancestors who lived right here in Fortune's Well. *Should I shout at him? Stand my ground? Should I reason with him, talk it out, stay calm? What girl will I be when I walk into that room?*

'Come in.'

I swallow hard, the handle turning in my hand and then I'm inside, facing him. My mind goes blank. He has his back to me, stuffing a load of files into a box on the floor. On the desk an old microscope stands proudly; I remember it from years ago when I took it into school for show and tell. I was so proud of my father, the scientist. I remember wanting to work in a lab when I grew up, just like he did. I wonder now where that girl has gone. Next to the microscope are a few vials and containers with swabs inside. Beside them, a pile of something that looks a lot like bloody tissues.

'Dad, are you okay?' I nod towards the bundle and he swiftly grabs at it with gloved hands and places it somewhere behind the desk.

'I'm fine, sweetheart. Just cut my finger earlier that's all.' He wipes his sleeve across his sweating brow and flashes me a smile. 'Everything alright?'

'Yeah, I'm just heading out to the library…'

'The library, huh? Even during summer, we can't pull you away from those books.' He pulls off his gloves and throws them into the wastepaper basket. I notice he doesn't seem to be wearing a Band-Aid. *Strange.*

'I guess so.' I smile back. 'I'm meeting JJ there.'

His head snaps up. 'Ah, young Mr Carson. Say hello to him for me.'

'I'll do that.'

'He's a good kid, Darcie… You would let me know if he were having any difficulty at home, wouldn't you? If anything strange was going on?'

'JJ's fine, Dad.'

'Oh, I'm sure he is. I just worry. A kid like that all alone with an alcoholic uncle. Must be tough.'

'Must be…' I step back out of the room and give him a little wave, 'anyway, I gotta shoot, so…'

'See you soon, sweetheart,' he grins.

*

My heart pounds like a drum the entire way to the library. *Why am I so nervous?* I pull open the heavy doors and find a space at the back, spreading the copy of the article out on the desk in front of me. I'm still not entirely sure if this will help us in any way, but at least having a bit more knowledge about the hangman will help us understand him.

Perhaps even destroy him. I lean back on my chair so that I can see the front of the library through a gap in one of the shelves, until an assistant comes along and begins to fill the void with new volumes. I place my headphones in and wait, getting to my feet and pacing back and forth, biting my lip. The words of Church by Aly & AJ flood my ears, calming me. Then I see him, JJ Carson, the boy from the river, moving in from the glaring sunshine outside and making his way across to me, beaming from ear to ear. His right eye is swollen and black and I instantly tense, remembering my father's words.

'Hey,' I pull the headphones from my ears and place an arm on his. 'What happened to your eye?'

'Oh,' he looks surprised, as if he has forgotten all about it. 'It's nothing. I bumped into a wall. You okay?'

'Yeah, I'm fine. How are you? What happened with your mom?'

'It was pretty intense,' he sighs and takes a seat at the desk. I join him. 'She didn't exactly have all the answers, but she did tell me that she has powers too, so did my grandmother. We're not sure how far back in the family it goes.'

'So, your mom... she can...?' I glance down at his wrists.

'No, that was news to her too. She has a kind of extra sight; it's how she knew what was happening with my dad having an affair. That's why she...'

'Extra sight?'

'Yeah, she can see pictures in her head of what people have been doing so there's no point ever lying to her.' He lowers his eyes and chuckles softly. 'Now that I think about it, I never could get one over on her when I was a little kid. Somehow, she always knew what I'd been up to. Anyway,

199

my grandmother was like an empath or something. She could read minds. Pick up on feelings.'

'Wow.' I'm suddenly aware of how pathetic my response is but I have no idea what to say. This kind of stuff just doesn't happen. 'So, if your mom had the power of extra sight, how did that lead to her... You know.' I pound a fist into my open palm.

'She said she flew into a rage. Like something took over her.'

'Something... or someone?' I swivel the article around for him to read, and watch him, biting my lip as he adjusts his glasses and scans the words. He leans in closer to get a better look.

'The cottage in Fortune's Well along the river walk, gained its name for being the infamous home of the town's executioner, Isiah Moorcroft who was gifted the lodgings by the mayor for his many years of service...' JJ reads aloud then looks at me with a frown. 'That name rings a bell for some reason.'

'Moorcroft?'

'Yeah. I think so...'

'Could be a distant relative,' I shrug. 'If White was your mother's maiden name it would be because her mother married a White, but maybe *her* maiden name was Moorcroft. You said that cottage was in your family for generations, right?' He stares up at me wide-eyed then back to the page.

'After years of courting, the executioner was set to wed local farmer's daughter, Edith Jones. It was reported that after their meeting he grew soft and wished to retire with his wife and new baby girl. Shortly after the baby turned one, Jones was accused of conspiring against the local government and the executioner was forced to put his own wife to death.' JJ's face turns white and he slides the paper away.

'He was forced to kill her JJ. Then he turned on the town. He murdered half the officials, including the mayor before ending his own life. I bet you can't guess where...' He pushes the hair from his eyes and rubs a hand against his chin. 'He was heartbroken. Angry. Sound familiar?'

'So, what are you saying? His ghost is somehow lingering in that place? Latching on to anyone it can? That's not possible, ghosts aren't real.'

'And superpowers are?'

He takes off his glasses and wipes the lenses. There's a long pause. I want to reach out to touch him. His arm, his face, any of him and all of him. My fingers stretch out across the desk, but he doesn't notice, so I pull back immediately.

'So, what now?'

'Well, I think we go to your uncle maybe? Ask him what, if anything, he knows about the cottage? I'm guessing the baby inherited the house and you're related to her?'

'Right.' He pulls back his seat and holds out a hand to me. I take it and he pulls me up beside him. 'Let's go.'

We're back in the sunshine now, the sound of people rushing in and out of shops, the honking of car horns and chatter of birds. JJ sits at the bus stop with sketch pad in hand, scribbling away. It's such a nice day that normally I would suggest we walk, but we have to get to Henry, there will be plenty of other days for us to walk hand and hand along the river. *I hope.* Then I see the strangest thing across the street. It's Vicky Marshall, staring at me from a shop window. I wave but she doesn't respond, she just stands there, staring. As I step towards the curb, I notice my own reflection in the shop window standing right beside her. A dark figure looms behind her with a noose in hand. It weaves it around Vicky's neck and hurls her up, her legs kick out in panic as she claws at her throat.

'Vicky!' I cry out, taking a step off the curb and making a run for her. A deep honking sound hits my ears, and a hand pulls me back onto the safety of the pavement.

'Darcie! What the hell? You could have got yourself killed!' JJ pulls me in to him and shakes my shoulders. I peer across the street at the shop window, but there is now no sign of my friend or the hangman. Just some poorly dressed mannequins. 'Darcie, Darcie can you hear me? You almost got hit! What is it? What's wrong?'

'It's Vicky,' I utter, turning to face him. 'I think she needs our help.'

35: JJ

Darcie looks grey with fear and she's shaking hard as I pull her back into my chest and wrap my arms tightly around her. Just then the bus pulls up and Darcie steps back, shaking her head as if trying to dislodge the image of whatever spooked her so badly.

'What did you see?'

'Vicky,' she gulps, glancing nervously at the shops across the street. 'In the shop window over there, but it wasn't really her.' She looks back at me and lowers her voice as the people start to flood past us to climb on the bus. 'The hangman had her,' she hisses into my ear, her breath warm on my neck. 'I think it was a vision. I don't know.'

I hold on to her shoulders. 'Has this happened before?'

'Yes,' she nods, sighing heavily. 'I keep seeing her, JJ. Vicky in trouble, but she's not really there. It's like the hangman is taunting me or warning me. He'll hurt her if we don't stop digging.'

I nod at the bus and pull out some coins. 'C'mon, let's go. You want to see her?'

'Let me try calling her.'

I pay our fares and we make our way to the back of the bus where we huddle in the corner next to the window. I almost slip an arm around her shoulders as she crosses one leg over the other and hunches over her phone. But I don't. We're not like that. Are we?

Darcie holds the phone to her ear and frowns at me, waiting. Then, her face lights up and her free hand grips my knee. 'Vicky! You okay?'

They talk for a few minutes before Darcie hangs up and slips the phone back into her pocket. She tucks her loose hair behind her ears, making me wonder what happened to the polished ponytail today. I run my eyes over the scruffy hoodie and remember her battered face in the hospital that day. What is happening to her?

'She's fine,' Darcie breathes out in relief. 'She said something about meeting up later.'

'I'm glad she's okay,' I nod, but am I? Something in my belly tightens, spreading tension up my spine and into my shoulders where there should be relief that Vicky is all right. I roll my shoulders, swallow, and turn to Darcie. 'What do you want to do?'

'See Henry,' she replies. 'He must know more about the cottage. Did your mom not know anything of the history?'

'Nope, nothing. Neither did her mum.'

'I'd like to dig up a full family tree on her side,' Darcie breathes out slowly, and leans back for a moment, her eyes glazed over as she stares out of the window.

'It's my cottage,' I tell her then. It slips out before I can stop it but once I've said it, I am glad. I need Darcie. I need her to help me and she can only help me if she knows everything.

'What?' she presses against me, her breath puffing against my cheek. Again, I feel the urge to slip an arm around her, hold her tightly to me but something stops me. 'Are you serious?'

'Uncle Henry gave me a box,' I explain. 'I'll show you when we get there. It had my birth certificate in it, old baby stuff, that kind of thing. *And* the deeds to Hangman's Cottage which becomes mine on my eighteenth birthday.'

Darcie stiffens. She swallows slowly and the colour drains from her face once again. She eases herself away from me and lifts her hand from my knee.

'What?' I ask her.

'You're smiling,' she says, in a whisper.

*

When we get to the farm, we find Uncle Henry sitting in one of his sagging deck chairs in the front yard, with Chester at his feet. He lifts a beer as we approach with caution. Drinking again. Not a good sign. My hand strays towards Darcie's and then retracts. What did she mean about me smiling? In that moment, I swear, she looked afraid of me.

'Hello young folk!' Uncle Henry bellows, swigging from the beer and leaning over his knees. He manages to sway even though he is sitting down. 'And how are you on this fine, sunny day?' His bloodshot eyes roll up to the calm blue sky and he grins in triumph. 'Absolutely beautiful, my beauties!'

Darcie nudges me and lowers her head. 'We're not gonna get much sense out of him.'

'He probably doesn't know anything anyway,' I shrug.

'Gonna make me a coffee, JJ?' Uncle Henry asks as we stop beside him. 'Think I might need a coffee.'

'Yeah, sure,' I agree and hold out my hand. 'You coming in?'

'Well, why not?' he beams happily and grabs my hand. It takes some effort to haul him up out of that deck chair and Darcie has to grab my other arm to stop me tumbling into his lap, but we do it. And Uncle Henry lolls against me, wrapping an arm around my shoulders as we plod steadily into the house. 'I'm sorry about that,' he says as the door slams behind Darcie. He reaches for my face and gently caresses my swollen eye. 'I'm really sorry about that, JJ. I never should have done that.'

'You hit him?' Darcie exclaims from behind.

'It wasn't like that,' I explain quickly and herd Uncle Henry into the nearest chair. He tumbles into it and rests his head back, his eyes half-slitted while his smile fades.

Darcie stands by the door, arms folded tightly, glaring hard at Uncle Henry. 'You said you bumped into a wall.'

'Forget about it!' I practically shout at her. She flinches, narrows her eyes and says nothing. 'Can you make him a coffee?' I ask her. To this, she rolls her eyes dramatically, tosses her hair and marches into the kitchen without a word.

'*Feisty*,' Uncle Henry nods approvingly, watching her go. 'I like her.'

'Me too,' I mutter, perching on the arm of the chair next to him. 'Uncle Henry, can we please talk to you?'

'Yep,' he laughs and waves a hand in the air. 'Speak. Speak your mind!'

'It's about Hangman's Cottage and my mother's family.'

The smile drops away in an instant. Uncle Henry lifts the beer to his lips and drains the last mouthful, while his eyes shift from me and drift to a photo on the mantel. He and my dad, arm in arm, teenagers sitting up on a great big green tractor.

'What about it?' he murmurs.

Darcie strolls back in and hands him a coffee without a single word. She returns to the door and stations herself in front of it with her arms crossed. She is not happy with either of us. Not one little bit.

Christ. I rub my face and look back at Henry in

despair. 'Didn't you say it was in her family for generations?'

He lifts and drops his big shoulders. 'Maybe. Dunno. Don't care.'

'Do you know anything about the original hangman who first lived there?'

'No,' he gives a slight shake of his head. 'I didn't know there was one.'

'Yeah, a real one. The town gave him the cottage to thank him for his services.'

Uncle Henry chuckles softly. 'Must have been one hell of a guy.' His eyes shoot to me and he frowns. 'He's related to you?'

Now it's my turn to shrug. 'We think so.'

'We've been doing some research,' Darcie finally speaks up. 'The story wasn't that hard to find, but it's kind of weird how no one ever talks about it.'

'Maybe because it was hundreds of years ago?' Henry suggests with a roll of his eyes.

'Maybe,' Darcie replies. 'Maybe the town were embarrassed of the way they treated him and never spoke of it again.'

'Why? What'd they do to him?'

'Accused his beloved wife of conspiring against the government and forced him to hang her,' Darcie tells him with a strange look of triumph in her eyes. She glances at me and I wait for a smile or a nod, but she is still pissed off. She walks slowly over to Uncle Henry and stands right in front of him. 'After that, the guy went a bit feral. He murdered half the town by the sounds of it.'

Uncle Henry looks a bit grey. He sips the coffee, squirms in the chair and glances at me with a grimace. 'Shit.'

'Do you believe in ghosts?' Darcie barks at him then.

He flinches. 'Ghosts? Is that what this is about?' A dark look passes over his face and he sucks in air as if preparing for battle. 'Ghosts and spirits and family curses, eh? Is that it, JJ?' Now his angry glare is solely on me. 'That the kind of bullshit your crazy mother filled your head with when you saw her, hey?'

I swap a cautious look with Darcie and she steps back, arms still tightly around her middle.

'No,' I shake my head. 'It wasn't like that. *We* know more than she does, *we-*'

'You're clutching at straws!' he yells at me and drops his head briefly into his hands. 'Trying to justify it, trying to make excuses for it when there ain't any!'

When he looks back up, I can see the terrible conflict in his eyes. He wants to get mad, he wants to scream and yell, he wants to hurl the coffee at the wall and tell me to get the hell out of his house. But he also wants to contain it, he wants to be better, he wants me to have a chance. I can see it all and it breaks my heart. I look at Darcie, catch her eye and jerk my head towards the door. She nods and opens it, planning our escape.

'Forget it,' I tell him, slipping off the arm of the chair and holding both hands up in surrender. 'We just wanted to know if you knew anything about the history of the cottage, that's all.'

'I'll tell you what I know,' he growls then. 'When I was a kid, when we were growing up here, everyone said to stay the hell away from that creepy place. To stay the hell away from the White women, who were probably witches! That's what people said. They said bad luck and bad decisions followed that family around.' He shakes his head at me, looking me briefly up and down in something that resembles disgust. 'They weren't right in the head, that's what people said. And they were right, weren't they, eh? Because my brother got mixed up with Cora and look what the hell happened to him!'

I swivel away from him, stony faced. 'Let's go.'

Darcie follows me out of the house and the door slams behind us. Inside, I hear the coffee cup explode against the wall and Uncle Henry roars for all the world to hear:

'That *bitch* murdered my brother, and you want to blame *ghosts!*

36: Darcie

'Um… What the fuck is that?' JJ asks.

'It's probably just a dead mouse or something,' I call back.

'It's moving.'

'Is it?... Holy shit!'

Whatever it is I smack it with an old shoe, and it scurries away, its feet pattering against the dusty floorboards. I wait until my breathing returns to normal before turning back to JJ. 'Little more light, please.'

'Remind me why we're up here again.'

'You'll see.' I stumble across the attic floor on all fours, ripping open boxes and rooting around inside, before moving on to the next. 'You trust me, right?'

'I suppose I have to.'

'What's that supposed to mean?'

'You're just very… *determined* when you're on a mission.'

'Jeremy said he thought it was right back here… Ah!'

'Is it that thing again?'

'Nope, found it!'

I crawl back towards the hatch and pass a small box down to JJ. He takes it with one hand and uses the other to steady the ladder for my descent, his eyes not knowing where to look. With my feet safely back on the ground I dust off my jeans and smile up at his red face. He hands me the box and lifts the base of the ladder, struggling to push it back up into the ceiling. With a smirk I reach out and flip the catch on the side, and for a moment I worry he's going to fly up with it.

'Something your uncle said back at the farm got me thinking,' I begin, as we return to my room and perch on the rug. I place the box in front of me and begin to unpack it.

'If it's about my eye, it's fine. I know you're pissed but-'

'It's not about your eye. But you're right... I *am* pissed.' He recoils slightly, like a scared schoolboy. I make a mental note not to be so hard on him. 'It was something he said when we left about blaming ghosts. Clearly the hangman has something he wants to tell me, so I think it's time we let him talk.' I proudly place the item on the floor in front of me.

'A Ouija board, really?'

'Really,' I grin. 'Grab your coat.'

'Why? Where are we going?'

'Your cottage, of course.'

*

JJ waits outside as I go to find my family in the kitchen. Ever since I have been less invisible Mom likes to know where I am at all times. Probably worried I'll end up like Jared Wheeler, or worse. She's baking with Julia and I can't help but wonder why she ever hired a housekeeper in the first place. Don't get me wrong, I love Julia, she's family, but my mother likes to micromanage everything and usually ends up doing it all herself. When I tell her where I'm going my dad peers around from the counter where he's painting Warhammer figurines with Jeremy. I'm almost free when he catches me at the door before I leave.

'Sweetheart,' he peers off into the other room, making sure we are alone. 'I have to ask before you go. JJ's eye...'

'What about it?'

'I think you know, young lady.' *Young lady?* 'Do you happen to know how he got that banged up?'

'Andrew and Frankie, they-'

'No, no, no. I saw those boys, they were useless against him and he didn't have a black eye when I took him to the hospital.' He rubs a hand across his stubbled chin. 'Did Henry Carson do that to him? You can tell me.' I reach for the handle, but he grabs my hand. 'Sweetheart.' He peers down at me, brow furrowed. I stare down at my feet, back into the other room, then up at him and nod, biting my lip. He nods back and steps aside, allowing me to exit. JJ looks up at me from the bottom of the steps as I leave, looking a little frustrated.

'What took you so long?'

'Sorry, my dad was being weird.' *It seems to be a habit of his lately.* I still haven't told JJ about the files, with so much already going on, the last thing I want is him being even more paranoid. Especially around my dad. It might mean he won't want me around anymore...

'Weird?'

'Just overprotective dad stuff, y'know?' His face drops. *Oh shit.* 'Sorry, I didn't mean... He asked me about your eye.'

'Did you tell him how it happened?' He peers up at the windows and rubs the back of his neck.

'No,' I smile. He seems relieved by this, and I suppose technically I haven't lied. Not really.

*

When we reach the building along the river it's just as horrifying as ever. The weeds have gotten worse, twisting their way up towards the windowsills, and the grey bricks seem to shift and crumble just by me looking at them. JJ performs the usual routine, breaking in through the back and coming around to heave the heavy front door open for me. My palms begin to sweat when he takes longer than usual and my stomach ties in knots, but then I hear the crunch of his footsteps from the other side of the wood.

'Holy shit,' I gasp as I step into the ominous hallway. The floor is littered with glass, broken china, and splinters of wood. In the kitchen all the drawers are yanked out and upturned on the floor, and some of the cupboard doors hang on for dear life at the hinges. 'What the hell happened in here?'

'Long story.' He clears a space in the small living area, and drags a wooden cabinet across the floor, plonking it in the middle of the two sagging armchairs. 'Will this do?'

I nod and place the board on top of the cabinet. 'Have you got any candles?'

'Is that a séance thing or...?'

'It's an I can barely see my hand in front of my face in here thing,' I laugh. Although the sun is still full and bright outside, the windows that remain intact are so damn greasy that there's no way any light can break through. They may as well be painted over. JJ lights a few candles and takes the seat opposite me, sinking back into the fabric. Our eyes meet across the candlelit room and I feel myself smiling.

He smiles back goofily. 'What?'

'Nothing. Let's start.'

I place the planchette on the board and put my pointer finger on it, gesturing for JJ to do the same. He hesitates but slowly inches forward until his finger connects with the smooth edges. His eyes dart up at me and I see his Adam's apple quiver as he gulps.

'Now what? Nothing's happened.'

'We're supposed to ask it questions.' It feels weird using this old board again. Jeremy and I used to be obsessed with it when we were kids, but after Jenna died, our parents stashed it away in the attic. Said it was morbid. Maybe they were right. I'd thought about using it a few times to try and contact Aunt Jenna, but I was always too afraid. To discover she was still here, floating around in some spirit form scared me. I like to remember her the way she was. Fiery and full of life.

'If you're there please give us a sign. Can you hear us?' I swear I feel the planchette shudder beneath my touch, but JJ is peering around the gloom, unnerved, and doesn't seem to have noticed. 'We know your story. We know what happened to your wife.' Once again, the planchette rocks and judders, only this time there's no doubt that JJ feels it too.

'No! Don't break the connection!' I reach out my free hand and grab hold of his wrist just in time to stop him from letting go. 'Please, tell us. What is it that you want?'

The planchette jolts across the board, taking our fingers with it.

'R... E... V...' JJ's eyes widen.

'Revenge.' I conclude as it circles the final letter. 'Revenge for what? You killed all those people, wasn't that enough? What more could you want?' The planchette moves across more letters, spelling out another word: *Bloodline.*

'So, that's it. He wants me and my family dead. That's why he made my mum go crazy all those years ago. That's right, isn't it? You want me gone?' JJ calls into the air but there's no answer.

'Wait, JJ. That can't be it. It just doesn't make sense. If he's one of your ancestors, why would he want revenge on you and your family?'

'If not us, then who? What the hell does *bloodline* mean?'

I rack my brain for an answer when a noise from outside steals my focus. My finger slips from the board. There's a banging on the door followed by a voice. Shit, it's Vicky Marshall.

'What the hell is *she* doing here?' JJ growls.

'She said she wanted to meet up, my parents must have told her I was with you,' I shrug helplessly at him. 'She must have followed us!'

Vicky's voice grows louder, and she begins hammering once again on the door. That's when I notice it, rising behind JJ's chair, just one hand at first, and then another. Clawing its way up from the ground—a huge dark mass. *But why now?* Vicky shouts again and the form begins to grow and shift. I let out a gasp as the realisation hits me.

'Vicky's family have lived here in Fortune's Well for years,' I whisper. 'The hangman may have killed the mayor, but what he really wanted was to take away the ones he loves. Destroy the bloodline. JJ, don't you get it? That's why you're so triggered around her. Her dad is the current mayor!'

Vicky's fist hits the door and I turn towards it, unsure whether to call her inside, scream for her to run, or ignore her entirely. I bite my lip and turn back to JJ for advice, but to my horror all I see before me is a deep, swirling cloud of darkness.

37: JJ

I'm me.

But I'm not me.

I'm filled up with cold…with emptiness. I feel nothing, not for Darcie, not for Uncle Henry, not for myself. It's like being a ghost, being dead and for some reason, the thought of that makes me laugh. I throw back my head as the sound rips out of me, spewing up out of my open throat and chilling the air around us.

I see Darcie - her mouth hanging open, her eyes wide like moons and I feel nothing. Nothing. She is no one. Nothing matters. You live, you die, you live, you die. Over and over again.

What is the point?

What is the point in anything?

These thoughts consume me as I find myself moving rapidly towards the door. Behind that door is Vicky Marshall and something about her, something about her name wants to poke me, stab me, pierce through me and it's like an itch I cannot scratch... Marshall, Marshall, Marshall…

'JJ!' Darcie screams as I approach her but I don't look at her, don't see her. She means nothing. But the banging on the door, on *my* door, on *my* cottage, cannot go on. It is thudding through my head, setting my brain on fire and I want to rip that door off the hinges and seize that interfering little bitch by her scrawny little neck!

And I know I can do it too. I can demolish that old door, turn it into wood-chips with just a flick of my hand and then Vicky Marshall is all mine. That will teach her, that will teach her to leave me and my family alone!

'Darcie, let me in!'

Oh no, I won't be letting you in, Vicky. There is no place for you here. But out there? Out there in the darkness there is a perfect place waiting for the likes of you. I smile, almost tenderly, as I push my arms out in front of me and send the mist towards the door. It rolls like black thunder, angry and tumultuous as it sends Darcie spiralling away and smacks into the door with a roaring rage and a delicious glee.

The wood explodes - jagged splinters flying everywhere. And there she is. Vicky Marshall, ducking down from the exploding wood, folding her arms over her head as if that is enough to protect her from me.

I move towards her quickly and I feel bigger than ever, I feel like I could fill the whole town if I wanted to and maybe I will, after this. Maybe I will roll through Fortune's Well, sending black smoke into every home, every building, every street. Maybe it's time they remembered me…

'No, JJ, *no!*' screams the girl behind me. I barely recall her name now. I am expanding. I am rolling and turning and clawing my way towards the girl who dared to hammer upon my door.

And she is turning, she is frightened and she is screaming and running, but she will not outrun me…

There she goes. Hair flying behind her like a cape as she thunders down the raggedy path towards the black coils of the waiting river. I roar with laughter and make my chase, and oh what a delicious chase it is. Me, versus her. The little girl, the mayor's daughter, fleeing for her pointless, stupid little life!

Run little girl, run! You'll make this so much more fun for me if you run!

'JJ, no, please, don't do this! JJ! It's not you! It's the hangman, don't let him!'

I sense her behind me but she is just a flea, just a bug, just a germ, she is nothing, she is no one and when I have executed the mayor's daughter I will turn around and squeeze the life out of her too.

The running girl attempts to turn a corner at the river path. I know what she is thinking. She plans to zig-zag out of sight, using the darkness as cover and she knows there are other gardens around here, places she can hide, people she can run to for help.

But no one is going to save you, Vicky Marshall, you worthless little whore!

I throw out a coil of mist and it loops around her ankles, sending her sprawling into the undergrowth. Panic grows on her pale face as it turns towards mine and suddenly, I am upon her, far quicker than she could have ever anticipated and she knows that all is lost. She knows that now she dies.

I cannot wait to see her swinging. I cannot wait to see her hands clawing at the rope. I cannot wait to watch her face turn purple as her eyes swell up in their sockets. I throw out another swirl of mist and this one spins around her neck, tightening instantly and lifting her clear off the ground.

She has no time to call out, no time to cry or scream or beg. She is just a rag doll, a nothing, no one, dead baby girl hanging in the air until the last of her breath is ripped from her body.

'*No! No!* JJ stop this! You have to fight him! You have to stop this!'

But it's too late. I don't know who she is anymore...

I don't remember who I am either. I fix my glare on the writhing girl caught in my noose and wait for her to die.

38: Darcie

Oh shit, oh shit, oh shit!

I climb to my feet and dust the splintered fragments from my hoodie. My head is spinning and something warm and sticky drips down my line of sight. It stings like lemon juice in an open wound when I dab at it with my fingers. *Ah!* But then I hear her scream—my friend, Vicky Marshall. It echoes across the riverbank, up through the twisted trees overhead and far across the fields. Without a second thought I hobble through the doorway as fast as I can. I must have twisted my ankle when JJ forced me back like that. No, not JJ, something else. Something primeval.

'No, JJ, *no!*' I'm crying out, and if he is still in there somewhere, he doesn't seem to hear me. I see Vicky up ahead, she's running for dear life, petrified and confused. The mist gains on her and if she couldn't see it before, she certainly can now! It's all because of him, that tormented soul from the cottage, that dark entity. She can see the mist now because it wants to be seen. He's tapped into JJ's powers somehow, using him like a puppet.

I can see him now, looming overheard, glued to JJ's back like a Siamese twin. He raises his huge arms and JJ's rise with them as if connected by a string. A thick, prickly tendril of mist shoots forward, weaving its way around Vicky's ankle and tugging her into the dirt. I know it must hurt her because her chin makes an awful crunching sound as it collides with the gravelly undergrowth.

I'm calling out, screaming for him to fight the darkness, for him to remember who he is, to save Vicky, himself, the town. I'm screaming anything and everything I can, but it all goes unheard. Now I'm just like the girl banging on the glass of the mirror, trapped inside of a nightmare which I may never wake up from. A foggy noose weaves its way around my friend's neck, hurling her up into the treetops and pulling tighter, and tighter, and I watch on in horror, screaming out over and over as her skin turns to a grey-blue colour, and her fingers desperately claw at her throat, her legs kicking out wildly beneath her.

'No!' I charge forward with all the strength I can muster, head pounding, ankle throbbing. I begin tearing through the bulbous black cloud that is growing, swirling like a twister before me. I see JJ's face through the frantic darkness, I see him facing towards the town with a grin and I know that once he's done with Vicky, Fortune's Well is next. As I push forward, palms outstretched I notice the strangest sensation. When I loop my fingers around the black tendrils they fizzle out and dissipate, before reforming again elsewhere. A soft glow emanates from my fingertips, it feels warm like a hot cup of cocoa, and tingles like pins and needles. I stare down at my hands in shock, then I hear the final breaths of Vicky rattling out of her taught, bruised throat.

I rush forward snatching at the mist, grabbing at every single piece of it I can. Pulling and ripping, and where it reforms, I swing my fists through it until it flickers out enough for me to reach her. I snatch at a tendril and it releases her to the ground where I begin clawing at the noose around her neck. She coughs and heaves as fresh air enters her lungs. There's a shadow over us now. It's him. JJ. The hangman. Whatever. It's standing over us and I hold her in my arms on the ground as it laughs, head thrown back, jaws wide.

'JJ, please! Please don't do this! I *love* you!' The words just spill out and I don't have time to recover, to take them back, swallow them and pretend they were never said. JJ's blank eyes change then, there's a flicker of something human in them. Something real. 'JJ… Please… Don't do this.' I'm shaking now and Vicky's passed out in my arms. 'Please.'

He looks up at the shadow above him and grits his teeth, arms outstretched and palms facing the sky. There's so much mist in the air you'd think that it were nightfall, a far cry from the warm early evening sun just a few minutes ago. His body begins to quake, and he cries out in agony. You think you've seen it all before, in the horror movies, people crying out in pain. But nothing prepares you for the real thing. Nothing prepares you for that awful ripping sound that tears from deep within the chasm of someone's very soul. The hangman's shadow begins to tremble, and the mist is slowly inching back inside of him, but he can't hold it for long. I know that, he knows that. I can see it in his eyes.

The hangman roars out into the sky and then he turns on JJ, pushing down on him creating a whirlwind of smoke. It causes the river to slop and splash and limbs to snap from the trees and begin swirling around him like a vortex, smacking against his face and ripping his clothes. His glasses crack. His hair looks almost white. This is it. This is the end. I lay Vicky's head down on the grass and peer up at the boy writhing in pain before me, the boy from the river, *my boy*. I crawl towards him, wind and debris knocking me back, but I won't give in, I just keep going, I have to get to him. I have to be with him when it ends.

I finally reach him and throw my arms around his waist; I can see now that he's crying, and I am pretty sure that I am too. Even through his clothes, his body feels like a jagged block of ice. I pull him tighter, the tingling in my hands warming him, but not enough… No way near enough.

'Darcie. Run,' he manages through gritted teeth.

'I can't, and I won't.' I grab his face in my hands, 'It's you and me, until the end.' I pull his face towards mine and our lips connect. Finally, after all this time. All the moments we've spent alone. All the obstacles we've faced. Finally, it is just me and him, and nothing else matters, the world outside can fade away. When I open my eyes, a warm golden light is oozing out of me like honey, it creates a shield around us and we shine together, burning like a star. The hangman croaks out one final cry as he shatters into a million tiny pieces and dissolves into the air. As he leaves, the mist retracts, as does the stunning golden hue surrounding us.

'What was… How did you?'

'I don't know…' I look down at my hands and up into his eyes.

There's a groaning noise from across the way and Vicky attempts to push herself upright with one hand, the other wiping at her eyes. I run over to help her.

'Vicky! Oh, thank God!'

'DeeDee? What the? What happened?' *She doesn't remember?* I glance back at JJ and he shrugs at me, a little unsure of what to do. I can see the old building in the distance behind him and I remember the smashed-up rooms and the exploding front door. 'There was a gas leak at the cottage. You could have been killed!' I haul her up from the ground and JJ nods at me, impressed by my quick thinking. I suppose, really, I am partially telling the truth. Vicky drops an arm around my shoulder, and we begin walking back towards the town. 'C'mon, we better get you checked out.' To my surprise JJ grabs her other arm and loops it around his neck. I notice she goes to say something but stops herself, instead flashing him a grin.

'Thank you,' I mouth to him behind her back. 'And about that other thing, what I said back there…'

'I know,' he smiles, and I smile back at him.

39: JJ

We walk Vicky to the hospital and drop her off in the A and E department. Darcie tries to insist on staying with her, but Vicky keeps shaking her head and waving her away. She looks different. Pale and drawn, her eyes lost and confused. I feel a surge of guilt and swallow it down.

I didn't hurt her. It was the Hangman.

'I'll be fine,' Vicky says again, smiling weakly as she waves her phone in Darcie's face. 'Mum is on the way. Go on, get out of here.'

'If you're sure? You've had such a shock.'

Vicky leans heavily against the wall as she waits her turn to be signed in. She looks up from her phone and her gaze shifts uneasily between me and Darcie.

'Seriously, I don't even remember a thing. Let alone a bloody explosion.' She shrugs helplessly and looks back down at her phone. 'Go on, I'll be fine.'

We turn away reluctantly and when we are out of sight, Darcie's hand creeps into mine. I fold my fingers over hers and hang on tight.

'She doesn't remember anything,' Darcie sighs, as we head wearily towards the farm.

'Thank God, imagine if she did?'

'Well I guess no one would believe her,' Darcie meets my eye and smiles. She looks done in, but the smile touches her eyes and I remember that golden glow that oozed out of her in the hangman's final moments. Her hand is soft and warm in mine and I want to hang on to it forever. I want to press my cold body against hers and let all her goodness, all her light seep into me and take me over. I never want to be cold and empty again.

225

'No one would believe any of us,' I nod and we walk on, our hands linked and swinging gently between us. 'So what do you think? It's over? Hangman and the mist?'

She exhales slowly, pushing out her lips and shaking her head slightly. 'I don't know, JJ. I hope so. I think so. How do you feel now?'

'Good,' I blink, almost unable to believe it. 'I feel good. Different. I don't know what the hell happened...but I think you saved me, Darcie. How the hell did you do it?'

'I have no clue,' she yawns in reply. 'I didn't exactly think it through at the time. I just didn't want him to take you. I didn't want to leave you.'

'Super brave crazy girl,' I laugh softly and she turns to me with another gentle smile.

'Yeah, maybe.'

'That light though...'

She nods. 'I know.'

'I think you're special, Darcie. Serious.'

Darcie tilts her head to one side as if considering this. 'Maybe we both are.'

We keep walking, almost home now, almost back to the farm and Uncle Henry. And I feel different. Brand new. A born-again JJ with something to live for. I feel bigger somehow. Stronger. Like all my broken pieces have joined up again, thanks to Darcie. She is my saviour. She is my everything. I feel shuddery when I look at her and my cheeks glow with warmth when I remember that kiss...

'I found out something recently. Both our families originate from here,' she murmurs sleepily as we trudge along, side by side. 'Do you ever wonder JJ? If there's something special about Fortune's Well?'

I can't help but laugh. 'You already sound like you want to start digging,' I joke.

'It's just… it almost feels like fate sometimes. That we met and went through all this stuff together. Your mist and that light and…' Darcie trails off, shrugging. 'I don't know.'

'There's not much summer left before school,' I remind her as the farm comes into view. 'But we could dig around a bit if you want to. Anyone else would want to put the whole thing behind them and never think about it again.'

'Super brave crazy girl,' she looks at me and winks.

I wink back and that's when I know I have to kiss her again. I just have to. Not an almost-kiss. Not a saviour kiss. A real kiss, between me and her. Right here. Right now. I pull on her hand and she slows to a stop and frowns at me, a soft smile on her lips. I'm grinning as I stare into her eyes and I wish I had some really awesome line to say to her, something really cool and memorable, something funny or sexy, but I don't. I don't have any words. But as soon as I'm home I'm going to get out my notebook and draw Darcie Duffield.

My other hand reaches for her arm and I pull her in close. She yields to my touch, her body weak with exhaustion. There are tiny splinters of wood in her hair, so I reach out and brush them away and my hand trails down to her cheek and I cup her face and lead it to mine. It's like a dream. I close my eyes and so does she and when our lips connect this time it feels just like coming home.

'JJ Carson?'

We yank apart in surprise. A tall woman in a navy-blue suit is striding up to the farmyard gate. Her dark brown hair is curled into a high bun and she has a black satchel on one shoulder and a file stuffed with papers under one arm.

I frown at Darcie, not understanding. 'Yeah?'

'My name is Sophie Stone, I'm a social worker from

Children's Services.' She flashes me a smile and extends a hand with bright red nails.

I don't take it. I gulp in fear and edge past her, my hand slipping away from Darcie. There are two cars parked in the yard and one is a police car. What the hell?

'What's going on?' I hear Darcie ask.

'Where's my uncle?' I glare at the woman as she falls into step with me.

'JJ, I know this is terribly unexpected and confusing but I'm going to have to ask you to come with me.'

I stop walking. 'What? Why?'

'Let me explain,' she tries to take me by the arm but I pull away and step back. 'There have been several complaints made against your uncle, Henry Carson. I'm afraid he's under arrest and the police are here to take him to the station. You're going to have to come with me.'

'What are you talking about?' I turn and march away, heading for the house. 'What complaints?'

The door opens then and two policemen come out with Uncle Henry between them. He's not in cuffs, but they are holding his arms and his head is hanging in shame. His hair is a shaggy mess, his clothes crumpled and stained. He looks like he's been on an even bigger bender since me and Darcie left earlier.

'Uncle Henry!' I call out and start to run, but the woman grabs my arm and holds me back.

'I'm sorry, JJ, I can't let you do that. It's for your own good. I've already packed you some things so if you just come and get in the car with me.'

Uncle Henry lifts his head long enough to see me. He doesn't say a word. He looks wretched and defeated as they herd him into the police car and slam the door on him. The engine starts and as the car pulls away, I turn to face the woman angrily.

'What the hell is going on? What complaints? What's he supposed to have done?'

She takes my arm yet again, leading me towards a waiting dark green Mini. I yank my arm away again and for the first time I look at Darcie. She's been awfully quiet, I think. And when I look at her, I think I know why. She is staring at her feet, biting at her lip, her brow furrowed, her shoulders hunched.

'There are a number of complaints including being drunk and disorderly in a public place, driving under the influence and operating farm machinery under the influence but the main ones are child endangerment, child neglect and child abuse.' Sophie Stone reels them off reluctantly and opens the passenger side of the door. 'I'm sorry, JJ, I really am. We want to hear your side of the story but right now, we have to do our job and it is not deemed safe for you to be here with your uncle.'

I shake my head at her, unable to digest what she is saying. 'Child abuse? Are you kidding me? That's a load of shit!'

'How did you hurt your eye?' she asks, tenderly and again when I glare at Darcie, she refuses to look back at me. Her eyes burn into her shoes as if she wishes the ground would open up and swallow her.

'Darcie,' I say through clenched teeth. 'What the hell have you done?'

'It's not just that,' Sophie says quickly. 'The school have a file of concerns about you, JJ. Poor attendance, consistent lateness, lack of proper equipment and uniform, inability to concentrate and a catalogue of minor injuries.'

'What?' I look back at her dazed, but then I remember. The years of hassle and assault from Jared Wheeler and his bastard friends.

I glare back at Darcie. 'What the hell did you do?'

She finally looks at me and tears fill her eyes. 'JJ, I'm sorry…'

I shake my head. My heart turns to stone. 'No, forget it,' I say and I turn around and climb into the social worker's car. She closes the door on me and says something to Darcie, before rubbing her shoulder and striding around to the driver's door.

My eyes meet Darcie's through the window and she is crying, but it's too late. I can't believe she did this. I stare her down and shake my head at her firmly so that she understands what she's done. She had no right to go meddling behind my back. I feel so betrayed, so angry, it's all I can do to contain myself. She stares back at me, her eyes swimming with tears and I shake my head at her again, then lower my eyes. It's over. As far as I'm concerned, our friendship is done.

End

Fortune's Well, Book Two:
Project Pandora
(Teaser)

JJ

I hear voices but I can't open my eyes. My eyelids are so heavy they feel like they have been glued shut. My head too, it's so heavy I can't move it or lift it. It feels like my entire body has been weighed down by cement and I've been buried alive.

'We'll give him less next time,' a female voice is saying. 'The idea is to have him sedated, not comatose.'

'Can't say I'm not nervous,' a man responds. 'We have no idea how safe this is yet.'

'Have faith, Roland. And patience. I think he's waking up. His eyelids are fluttering.'

'His finger just twitched. Should I be worried?'

'Don't be ridiculous. Move around this side.'

I try to open my eyes, but I still can't. I wriggle my toes instead and then my fingers. But something is badly wrong. And now I'm scared to open my eyes. If I open my eyes, I will see the people standing over me and maybe this won't be some god-awful freaky dream, and maybe I am really in deep shit. If I open my eyes, it will be real.

'Get the tray. I'll start some obs.'

Footsteps move, but they don't go far. I hear the metallic clang of a tray followed by more footsteps. I am rigid with terror. Utter panic is now clawing up my throat and threatening to spew out. I can feel my skin trembling and it won't be long before whoever the hell these people are work out that I am fully awake and just pretending to be out.

Shit, shit, shit!

What the hell happened? I scramble backwards in my mind, clutching at whatever I can remember. Uncle Henry at the bandstand. Hope. Beans on toast. Taking the rubbish out. Calling Darcie. Shit! Did she pick up? Maybe she heard the whole thing. Maybe she has alerted Uncle Henry and the police and they are coming for me. Because this sure as hell is not the police station and those men in uniform were definitely not the police. Christ, what was I thinking?

The last thing I remember is the tall one with the sunglasses leaning over me to do up my seatbelt which was kind of weird because I'm not three…Then there was a pain in my arm. That was it. They did something to me.

Oh shit, oh *shit*, this is not good!

I feel something cold pushed into my ear and it takes all my control not to scream out in terror. There is a beat or two and then a loud beep.

'Temperature is 37.6.'

There is some rustling of paper and I can hear the scratching of a pen. I am struggling now. I want to pretend I am asleep but it's getting harder. I can feel my nostrils stretching and flaring as the terrified breath I am holding in tries to escape. There is a lump in my throat and a tremor behind it begging to be set free. I might scream. I might cry. I might piss my pants.

A fabric cuff is slipped around the top of my arm and tightened. I hold on, moving my lips just enough to bite down hard on my tongue. I can't let them know I'm awake. Maybe if I stay under, they will leave and then I can figure this thing out. I can use the mist to escape. Surely that's possible?

A pumping sound follows and the female voice announces: 'BP is a little high which suggests he is coming around from the sedative. Pass me the torch, Roland.' The blood pressure cuff relaxes and is removed and then suddenly cold fingers are pulling at my eyelids and prising them open. Instinctively, I turn my head but it's too late. The bright light is beamed into my eyes and I react as anyone would. They know.

'JJ Carson,' the female voice sounds, a note of triumph to her tone. She lowers the torch and I blink until my vision returns. I am staring up into the long, narrow face of a dark-haired woman in a white lab coat.

Not good. Not good at all. Darcie, please…

'It's good to see you awake,' the woman says, but her flat tone relays no joy or enthusiasm or interest in my welfare. I run my eyes quickly over her, picking up what details I can in case I need them later. She has high cheekbones. Her lips are thin, as is her nose. Her eyes are dark green and framed with lashings of thick black mascara. Other than that she wears no make-up and her hair is scraped back into a high bun. There are wrinkles around her eyes and mouth that suggest she might be in her fifties, but I'm no expert at guessing the ages of adults. Who the hell is she and what am I doing here?

'Take it easy,' a male voice advises so I shift my gaze to him. He is standing beside the woman, and I instantly recognise him as the 'cop' in the sunglasses. My stomach does a flip and I open my mouth, sucking in oxygen as my body begs me to panic. He has flint grey eyes and a hard mouth.

'What's going on?' I look back at the woman. 'Who are you? What did you do to me?'

'One question at a time,' she smiles, but there is no warmth in that smile, rather it looks like a pre-programmed reaction to being asked a question. 'My name is Erica Poole, and this is my colleague, Roland Mitchell. And you're here to help us, JJ. But there's plenty of time for that. How are you feeling right now?'

I look away from her taut, watchful face because it's giving me the creeps. I let my gaze drift around what I can see of my surroundings. The ceiling is white, as are the walls. I'm lying on a bed like the ones you see in hospital and along the same wall is a door. It has a small glass window and a security pad beside it. I try to sit up to get a better look and that's when I realise my wrists are secured to the bed with what look like metal clasps.

What the actual hell…?

Okay, now I'm panicking and there is nothing I can do about it. I struggle and jolt on the bed and glare up at the woman as she watches calmly. 'What is this? Why am I here? Get these the hell off me!'

'We can do that,' she nods, coolly. 'But you have to remain calm at all times, JJ. Do you know what a taser is?'

'*What?*'

'Roland.'

Roland holds up his hand for me to see that he is holding a taser. 'You don't want to know what this feels like, buddy,' he advises.

I look at Erica and she raises her eyebrows. 'Do we have an understanding? When I release the cuffs, you must always keep your arms at your sides. If you so much as lift a hand to wipe your nose or scratch your neck Roland is going to hit you with that thing and you'll wake up some time tomorrow. Got it?'

I swallow and nod. She leans over with a small metal key in her hand and sticks it into each metal clasp. I hear a series of clicks and each one falls open, releasing me. I sit up slowly, remembering to keep my arms down and my hands still.

'I don't know what this is about,' I tell her.

She laughs, and it's an atrocious sound. Cold and empty and mirthless in the small, echoey room. 'JJ, don't lie to us. That's rule number one. We know everything about you, and we know what you are capable of.'

I shake my head, lowering my feet to the floor. 'I'm not capable of anything. I'm no one. You've got the wrong person.'

She smiles graciously as if dealing with an infant and pulls a piece of paper from the file in her arms. She holds it up to read while Roland keeps the taser in my eye-line.

'JJ Carson, son of Cora White and the late James Carson. Cora White was also a person of interest for us until she got herself locked up. We know where you live, we know about your uncle, we know everything, JJ. And we know what you can do. We've been watching you for a very long time. Now, no more questions. I suppose you'd like the grand tour?'

I nod silently and make the decision there and then not to use the mist in front of these people. I must convince them they've got this wrong. So I slip off the bed and take deep breaths to stay calm.

I'm expecting them to head to the door, but they don't. Roland stands as close to me as he can get with the taser and Erica flings an arm at a toilet in the far-left corner of the room.

'There you have the bathroom,' she announces, before gesturing along the wall to a metal table and chair. They are both fixed to the floor and the wall. On the table is a plastic bowl with what looks like a hamburger in it and beside the bowl is a plastic cup with possibly coke in it. 'Dinner is served,' she says, staring at me while I take it all in. 'If you're hungry I suggest you eat it now, because we'll need to sedate you again in a minute. The same goes for the toilet.'

Now I'm pissed. 'You want me to take a piss in front of you?' I look wildly from one to the other and then the door. I seriously consider running for it but then I see the grim look on Roland's face as he waves the taser slowly in front of me.

'Up to you,' Erica shrugs.

'I'm not doing that.'

'Fine. Are you going to eat? I strongly advise you keep your strength up.'

'Why?' I glare at her intensely. 'What am I here for? What is this about?'

'You're not stupid, JJ, so don't pretend you are. You know very well what this is about and if you don't it won't take you long to figure it out. Are you going to eat?'

There is absolutely no way in hell I can eat a thing with them watching me. I shake my head. Erica nods at the bed. 'Very well then, let's get you settled back in.'

'Look this is a mistake, I'm telling you…' I try to bargain but Roland jabs the taser towards me and misses me by about an inch. 'You can't do this. Who are you people? You can't just take kids off the street. There'll be people looking for me!'

'Arms by your side,' Erica warns as I sit back on the bed. 'Lie down. This will all become very clear to you in time and I can assure you, eventually you will thank us. Now, until we figure out exactly what dosage of sedative keeps us safe from you but allows us to explore your abilities, you'll do exactly as we say. *Lie down.*'

With the taser so close I have no choice. Erica snaps the metal clasps back over my wrists and though it is tempting to release the mist and see if it can help me, something tells me not to let them know about it unless I really have to. There is a sudden sharp pain in my arm and I feel myself going back under. I close my eyes and fake heavy breathing, my head slumped to one side.

'Is he under?' Roland asks. 'That was quick.'

'Let's see…' Erica delivers a hard slap to my cheek, mashing my teeth against the inside of my mouth, but I don't react. I play dead. I want them to think they need to use a lower dosage on me. I release a tiny snore. 'We'll adjust it. Fifteen mils next time, I think. It needs to be just right. Docile and cooperative is what we're aiming for. Let's go.'

I listen to them leave the room but I don't open my eyes. In my fear and paranoia I imagine cameras blinking at me in the room. I need to keep up the pretence. Tears form in my eyes, escape and roll down my cheeks. I am shaking from head to toe. A few moments later I don't have to pretend anymore because the sedative takes me down and everything goes black.

To be continued…

Acknowledgments

Special thanks go out to our proofreader, Julie, for her keen eye for detail, and our beta readers (Leah & Rowan) for their vital feedback.

Thanks also to Luke Fielding for the amazing cover art, we are so grateful, and to all of our supporters.

Liked this book?

Please leave us a review on a platform of your choice.

Reviews can be as simple as a few words, and are important for authors as they help spread the word about books and allow other readers to find them.

We'd really appreciate seeing what you thought of this adventure.

Scan me with your phone camera
to review on Goodreads

About the Authors

Chantelle Atkins

Chantelle Atkins was born and raised in Dorset, England and still resides there now with her husband, four children and multiple pets. She is addicted to reading, writing and music and writes for both the young adult and adult genres. Her fiction is described as gritty, edgy and compelling.

Her debut Young Adult novel The Mess Of Me deals with eating disorders, self-harm, fractured families and first love. Her second novel, The Boy With The Thorn In His Side follows the musical journey of a young boy attempting to escape his brutal home life and has now been developed into a 5 book series. She is also the author of This Is Nowhere and award-winning dystopian, The Tree Of Rebels, plus a collection of short stories related to her novels called Bird People and Other Stories. The award-winning Elliot Pie's Guide To Human Nature was released through Pict Publishing in October 2018. YA novel A Song For Bill Robinson was released in December 2019 and is the first in a trilogy, followed by Emily's Baby and The Search For Summer in 2021. Chantelle has had multiple articles about writing published by Author's Publish magazine and runs her own Community Interest Company – Chasing Driftwood Writing Group.

www.ChantelleAtkins.com

Facebook @ChantelleAtkinsWriter

Twitter @ChanAtkins

Instagram @ChantelleAtkinsWriter

About the Authors

Sim Alec Sansford

Born and raised in the county town of Dorchester, Dorset, Sim began scribbling away stories on scraps of paper since before he can remember. He spent a lot of his childhood on adventures, walking the dogs in the woodland surrounding Thomas Hardy's cottage with his family. Something about the cottage and 'the man what wrote stuff' who had lived there sparked a fire inside him. It was from there he began to focus on writing more seriously.

In 2012, Sim signed up to Open University to study Creative Writing alongside working full time. He isn't quite sure how he made it out alive, but he graduated with honours and began using the skills he had acquired to edit and redraft old work.

Beginning his public writing career with a few short stories, his debut novel, Welcome to Denver Falls (Book One in the Denver Falls Saga) was published in August 2020.

www.SimAlecSansford.com

"I make words into adventures."
Sim Alec Sansford

Facbook @SimAlecSansford

Twitter @SimSansford

Instagram @Simeon_Alec

About Chasing Driftwood **Books**

Chasing Driftwood Books, established in 2021, is an off-shoot of Chasing Driftwood Writing Group, established in 2015.

Chasing Driftwood Books publishes fiction and non-fiction.

The first release being

Stay Home: A Year of Writing Through Lockdown

A collection of stories, poems, and essays from real people on their experience of the global pandemic.

The second collection will be titled

The World You Gave Us

A collection of stories, poems, and essays from young people aged 8+ about their thoughts, fears, and hopes for the world they live in now and the future we have left them. This collection is due for publication in late 2022.

Chasing Driftwood Writing Group runs various community driven creative projects, provides creative writing workshops for Children, Teens, and adults, and other writing related services such as editing, proofreading, formatting and marketing.

To learn more about us or for news and updates visit us online.

www.ChasingDriftwoodWritingGroup.org

Facebook @chasingdriftwood

Printed in Great Britain
by Amazon

80876249R00142